PU

SUPER
FIRE
STORM

Jake watched the forest floor uneasily. Every living creature seemed to be heading in one direction. The *opposite* direction to the one they were taking . . .

'I can smell the smoke,' Olly said. He coughed as if to prove his point.

Jake sniffed the heavy air a couple of times. He could smell smoke too, quite distinctly. And the orange glow ahead seemed to be spreading out.

It was much too wide to be the camp-fire.

Jake stopped and yanked on Olly's arm. 'Wait!'

The hair on the back of Jake's neck prickled.

'Ow!' cried Olly. 'What's up?'

Jake trembled. Now he understood why all the animals and insects were going the *other* way. And he realized, too, why were both coughing all of a sudden. 'That's not the camp-fire, Olly,' he cried. 'It's a *forest* fire.'

Some other books by Jack Dillon

SURVIVE! EARTHQUAKE ALERT
SURVIVE! HURRICANE HORROR

SURVIVE!

FIRE STORM

Jack Dillon

PUFFIN BOOKS

For Robin, Jo and Beth
Special thanks to Liss Norton and Ian Locke
Additional thanks to Nigel Russell

PUFFIN BOOKS

Published by the Penguin Group
Penguin Books Ltd, 27 Wrights Lane, London W8 5TZ, England
Penguin Putnam Inc., 375 Hudson Street, New York, New York 10014, USA
Penguin Books Australia Ltd, Ringwood, Victoria, Australia
Penguin Books Canada Ltd, 10 Alcorn Avenue, Toronto, Ontario, Canada M4V 3B2
Penguin Books (NZ) Ltd, Private Bag 102902, NSMC, Auckland, New Zealand

On the worldwide web at: www.penguin.com

Penguin Books Ltd, Registered Offices: Harmondsworth, Middlesex, England

First published 1999
1 3 5 7 9 10 8 6 4 2

Created by Working Partners Ltd, London W6 0QT

The moral right of the author has been asserted

Set in Bembo

Made and printed in England by Clays Ltd, St Ives plc

British Library Cataloguing in Publication Data
A CIP catalogue record for this book is available from the British Library

ISBN 0–140–38818–4

CHAPTER ONE

'Would you just look at all this!' Jake Weston said. 'Isn't it fantastic?' He was leaning over the rail of the river-boat *Santa Teresa*, gazing at the rain forest that grew right up to the banks of the river. It was like nothing he'd ever seen before. Huge trees stretched 30 to 40 metres into the sky. Below them, smaller palms and bright green plants with feathery fronds reached out over the dark water of the Rio Negro.

A macaw appeared in a sudden flash of scarlet and settled on a high branch, where it squawked, loudly and harshly. There was another answering call from deeper in the forest.

Olly, Jake's kid brother, joined him at the rail. 'I can hardly believe we're in Brazil.' Olly said, cleaning his glasses on his T-shirt. 'I hope we see some caymans.'

'As long as they don't get too close.'

'They're just like alligators, only their noses aren't so long, you know.' Olly put his glasses on again and peered hopefully into the black water. 'It says so in my book.'

Jake grinned. Olly had had his nose in a book all morning and his head was full of information he'd learned from his reading. Jake looked across at the rain forest again, marvelling at the height of the trees and the way every last centimetre of space was crammed with plants. It was lucky they'd have a guide to get them to the campsite, he thought. Finding your way through that lot would be pretty well impossible.

Olly nudged him. 'It says in my book that there's loads of snakes in Brazil.'

'Shut up, Olly.' Jake knew his brother was only saying it to wind him up. Jake was fascinated by every kind of animal – except snakes. He really hated them. Even looking at a picture of one sent shivers down his spine.

'Anacondas live in swamps and rivers,' Olly went on. 'They can be ten metres long.'

2

Jake felt a prickle of fear at the nape of his neck but he spoke calmly: 'So?'

'So, we might see one. There could be one swimming along by the boat right now, waiting to leap up and grab anyone who leans over too far.'

The chances of a giant snake being beside their boat were slim, Jake knew, but the idea was unnerving all the same. He drew back slightly from the rail, hoping Olly hadn't noticed.

His brother looked at his book. 'Cor, there's a whole load of stuff here about snakes. There's this other giant one that lives in the forest, a boa constrictor. It crushes you to death. And there's a red and yellow coral snake . . .' Laughing, he thrust the book in front of Jake's face, so he'd have to look at the pictures.

Jake pushed the book away. He caught Olly by the scruff of the neck and turned him round so they were facing the other passengers. They were an interesting mix: groups of young backpackers, families, older couples. Most people were talking or watching the scenery. A few were asleep, stretched out on benches or curled up on the wooden deck.

A family leaning on the rail on the opposite

side of the boat caught Jake's eye. There were five of them – parents, two long-haired boys a bit older than Jake and a girl who looked about Olly's age. 'That girl looks as though she needs a friend to play with,' Jake warned. 'If you don't shut up about snakes, I might just introduce you.'

Olly tried to prise Jake's fingers off his neck. 'Ow! You wouldn't.'

'Try me.'

Olly hated girls. He was always moaning about the girls in his class and Jake knew that his threat would make his brother shut up about snakes.

It did. When Jake let him go, Olly went and sat down with his book again.

Gill Weston, their mother, came along the deck towards them. She was a slim woman with mousy hair tied back in a pony-tail. 'Are you two fighting again?' She was smiling.

Jake grinned. 'Not us.' He winked at Olly. 'We never fight.'

Gill opened her rucksack and took out a bottle of water. 'Do either of you want a drink?'

Jake nodded and took the bottle. Though the sun was hidden behind thick clouds, it was unbearably hot. His T-shirt was sticking to him, as it had done since they'd got off the plane at Manaus, the capital of Brazil's Amazonas state.

'We'll be there soon, won't we?' he asked when he'd drunk a few mouthfuls of the tepid water. He could hardly wait to get off the boat and into the forest to look at the wildlife.

His bedroom at home in England was packed with pets – tropical fish, hamster, stick insects, ants that scurried through the tunnels of a formicarium. He even had a budgie that sometimes sat on his shoulder while he was doing his homework. But coming to the Brazilian rain forest was a dream come true. There'd be so many exotic animals to see here.

He looked out across the river again, just in time to see a troupe of spider monkeys come swinging, hand over hand, out of the trees. Fascinated, he watched them race back and forth alongside the river, chattering excitedly.

His mother looked at her watch. 'We should be there in about half an hour.'

'This is going to be the best holiday ever,' Jake said.

'It's hardly a holiday, Jake,' Gill reminded him.

Jake nodded. He knew there was a serious side to the trip. They were there to take part in a headline-grabbing invasion of a Logan Corporation lumber camp. The company, a huge multinational organization, had set up a logging operation in the heart of the forest and it was feared that they were ignoring quotas relating to the quantity and type of trees allowed to be cut down. Trees were being felled at such an alarming rate that people were travelling to Brazil from all over the world in protest and to try and stop them.

It was Gill who'd first heard about the demo. She was a freelance journalist, and the editor of a wildlife magazine had asked her to cover the story.

Jake had been eager to take part in the protest: the rain forest had to be protected. But going to Brazil would also give him the chance to see forest creatures in their natural environment.

Gill put the water bottle away and sat next to Olly. 'Aren't you tired, boys?'

Jake shook his head. He knew he should be tired. His mother and Olly had slept for a big chunk of the eleven and a half hour overnight flight from Heathrow to Rio de Janeiro, but Jake had barely slept at all. Not that he'd minded. He hadn't wanted to miss a moment of the flight. It was the first time he'd been on a plane and he'd loved every minute of it. Waiting at Rio airport for their connection to Manaus had been tedious though. Jake looked at his watch, trying to calculate the length of time they'd been travelling. 'It's nearly twenty-two hours since we left Heathrow,' he said at last.

'We must be mad,' his mother said, laughing. 'Coming all this way just to protest about a few trees being cut down.'

Jake knew she was joking. She was an ardent campaigner, always dragging Jake and Olly off to demonstrate about something or other during their school holidays. And usually she managed to fund their trips by selling a few magazine articles about the protests. Power stations, motorways, retail parks – over the past few years they'd tried to stop them all from being built.

Sarah, the girl Jake had sat next to on the bus from Manaus airport to the harbour, joined them. She was tall and skinny, with long dark hair and a cheerful smile. 'Did you see those monkeys back there?' she asked.

Jake nodded, enthusiastically. 'Sure did. Weren't they great?'

Olly looked up from his book. 'Did you know the world's deadliest spider lives in the

Brazilian rain forest? It's called a Brazilian wandering spider and it –'

'Quit it, Olly.' Jake said.

Olly smirked at him. 'I bet it could even kill a snake. Hang about, I think I saw a picture of one biting a snake earlier. I'll show you.' He began to leaf through the book.

Jake snatched it away and held it above his head.

'Give it back.' Olly jumped up in a vain attempt to reach it.

'Jake,' Gill said, frowning. 'Don't tease him.'

Jake laughed and handed the book back. 'One more word about snakes and I'll drop it over the side,' he warned.

Olly scowled at him.

'Look, there's a village,' Sarah called.

Jake moved to the side of the boat and leaned on the rail, trying not to think about the possibility of lurking anacondas. The village was a collection of corrugated-iron houses built on wooden rafts that stood on a wide sweep of black mud beside the river. They were so close together that it would be possible to walk from one end of the village to the other without getting muddy feet.

'They probably float in the rainy season, when the river's full,' Sarah said.

A group of brown-skinned, dark-haired children watched them go by, waving hard. Jake waved back. 'Imagine living out here,' he said. 'It's so remote and far away from the towns and cities. You'd never know what was happening in the rest of the world.'

'Yeah, I bet they don't have televisions,' Sarah said. 'What on earth do they do in the evening?'

Gill laughed. 'They probably talk to each other!'

The boat's engine note changed. 'We're slowing down,' Sarah said. She looked ahead. 'There's another boat. A big one.'

They came alongside the boat, rocking slightly in its wake. It was an old-fashioned paddle-steamer, painted white. People were sitting on long benches arranged along the sides of the boat. Most of them had cameras or binoculars slung round their necks. Behind them, the wide deck was full of hammocks.

'They must be tourists,' Gill said. 'Lucky things. Think of spending a week cruising along the Rio Negro.'

Jake pulled a face. 'I'd rather be trekking through the rain forest looking at sloths and jaguars.'

The *Santa Teresa* hooted twice, then speeded up again, leaving the paddle-steamer behind. Jake looked at his watch. 'Five or ten more minutes, I reckon,' he said.

Sarah moved away from the rail. 'I'd better go and find my mum and dad. I've left my backpack with them.'

'See you at the camp,' Jake said.

'Yeah. See you.'

Soon the boat began to head towards the bank. As they rounded a bend in the river, Jake saw a wooden jetty in front of them, jutting out into the water from the bank. A dark-skinned man with shoulder-length black hair stood on the jetty, watching the boat approach. He was dressed in khaki shorts, white T-shirt and walking boots. He smiled and waved as they drew near. '*Ola. Benvindo*,' he called. 'Hallo. Welcome. I'm here to take you to High Tree Camp.'

Behind him, an area of bank at the end of the jetty had been cleared to make way for a cluster of corrugated-iron shacks. A broad, muddy road led off into the forest. It was shimmering in the heat.

'Look at that,' Gill said, angrily. 'I bet the Logan Corporation made that road so they could get their heavy equipment into the forest.' She got out her camera and took some photos.

'All the rain forests will be wiped out in fifty years,' Olly announced.

'Exactly,' Gill said. 'That's why we need to do something. If it wasn't for people like us the Logan Corporation would flatten the entire forest.'

Jake nodded but he didn't say anything. He was too wrapped up in looking at the rain forest to get involved in a discussion now. They were close to the bank and he'd spotted a pair of huge, brilliantly coloured butterflies dancing round a purple flower on the edge of the forest.

The boat's engine throttled back and they drifted in towards the jetty. A crew member jumped off the back of the boat holding a rope. He wound it round a bollard, heaving on it until the boat was touching the jetty. A second crewman did the same at the front.

Passengers began to gather their bags and make their way to the side of the boat. Jake swung his rucksack on to his back. A thrill of anticipation ran through him. 'Here we go then.' He was about to set foot in a rain forest.

CHAPTER TWO

'**B**envindo,' the guide said, smiling broadly. He led the way down the jetty. 'Thank you for coming to join our demonstration. My name is Paulo.' He spoke with a strong Brazilian accent.

Everyone gathered round him, eager to be off. There were about fifty protesters from their boat – Europeans, Americans and some Brazilians from Rio. His mum had told Jake that other protesters would already have arrived at High Tree Camp, with more on their way. The logging-camp invasion was due to take place in a couple of days. With so many taking part, it was sure to be a success. They were bound to make the news all over the world and the pressure on the Logan Corporation to cease their forest demolition would be enormous.

'High Tree is about eight kilometres from here,' Paulo said. 'About a two-hour trek. It's easy to lose your way in the *selva* – the rain forest – so it's important to keep together. I will go in front. If you find you are falling behind, call out and I will wait for you to catch up.'

'Watch out for snakes, Jake!' Olly teased.

Jake pretended he hadn't heard. He didn't want to think about snakes. Trekking through a rain forest was going to be an experience of a lifetime and he wasn't going to let anything spoil it. Especially not his kid brother!

'Should we take any precautions?' an American woman asked. 'I was thinking about the jaguars.'

'Most rain forest animals will keep their distance,' Paulo said. 'I've lived in this area all my life and I've never seen a jaguar. But please don't pick up any insects. Some of them are venomous. And, above all, please don't smoke. The forest is very dry at this time of year. Follow me.' He set off along the rutted road.

Jake felt a momentary twinge of

disappointment. It would have been terrific to see a jaguar.

'Stay with me, Oliver,' Gill said. 'I don't want you wandering off and getting lost.'

Jake grinned. It was great being the oldest. His mum was usually too busy keeping an eye on Olly to worry about what he was getting up to. He spotted Sarah near the back of the group and made his way over to her. 'Can I walk with you?'

She smiled. 'You bet. I want to get as far away as possible from my little sister. All she does is whinge about being too hot.'

The group began to move. Jake and Sarah went with them, gripping the straps of their large backpacks . 'This is going to be fantastic,' Sarah said, smiling at Jake.

'I know. Brazil! I can hardly believe I'm really here.'

Sarah laughed. 'I meant the invasion, you idiot! We've got to stop the loggers.' She spoke passionately. 'People like them are destroying the world.'

To Jake's disappointment, they stayed on the road for the first kilometre or so. On either side of them, the rain forest looked dark, mysterious and fascinating and he was desperate to explore it.

After twenty minutes, Paulo stopped. He waited for everyone to catch up. 'This road leads all the way to High Tree Camp, where we've had a presence for the past two months. We've been collecting video evidence of the Logan Corporation operation and working out plans for the invasion. The road runs straight past the lumber camp, so we'll be making a detour. They know about our camp, but don't think we're much of a threat. We want to keep you a secret!'

'Have many other journalists arrived?' Gill asked. The protesters needed plenty of publicity if they were going to succeed in closing the lumber camp.

Paulo nodded. 'Yes, quite a lot. From magazines and newspapers world-wide and we're expecting TV crews from the USA, Britain, Japan and France tomorrow.'

Jake laughed. 'We're going to be on telly. We'll be famous!'

'And we're going to save the rain forest,' Sarah said. 'With this sort of media coverage, the Logan Corporation will have to pack up and go home.'

'We'll go into the forest now,' Paulo said. 'Please stick together. Don't allow yourselves to be left behind.'

A shiver of anticipation ran down Jake's spine. They were finally going into the forest.

Gill hurried back to Jake. 'Mind you keep up, won't you?'

'OK.'

She looked at him sharply. 'I mean it, Jake. The rain forest's dangerous if you don't know your way about.'

'I'll be careful.' Jake waited until she'd gone back to Olly. 'Mothers!'

Sarah laughed. 'Mine's just as bad.' She pointed into the group. 'Here she comes now.'

Sarah's mother looked like an older version of Sarah except that she wore her long, dark hair pinned up on the top of her head. 'Perhaps you should come with us now,' she said. 'Paulo said we should stick together.'

'I'll be fine with Jake, Mum. We won't get lost.'

Her mother looked doubtful.

'Really,' Sarah said. 'You don't need to worry about us.'

'All right. But make sure you keep up with the people in front of you.' She headed back the way she'd come.

'Honestly!' Sarah said. 'Parents treat you as though you're about five.'

'Follow me, then,' Paulo called.

The forest was dark.

That was the first thing that struck Jake. The vegetation was so lush and tall that very little light could penetrate to the forest floor. The second thing that struck him was the smell. The air was heavy with perfume. He sniffed, trying to locate the source.

'Up there.' Sarah was pointing above his head. He looked up. Part-way up a tree, a small bush was growing, its roots firmly anchored in the bark. The bush was dotted with deep crimson flowers. 'It's growing on the tree,' she said in amazement.

'It's an air plant,' Jake said. He'd found a whole web site about them on the internet. 'They get food from dust in the air and they catch water on their leaves.' He pointed out a white-flowered plant that wound through the branches of another tree. 'That's one, too.'

Walking in single file, they followed a narrow path that led them past more astonishing sights. They saw thick-stemmed grasses nearly 20 metres tall, tree ferns, palms with enormous leaves, flowers of every imaginable colour, some as big as dinner plates. Butterflies flitted through the occasional ray of sunshine that had somehow found a way through the thick canopy overhead.

The noise was amazing too. It went on incessantly: squawking, screeching, hooting, trilling, as though every bird in the forest was calling at once. Jake was entranced. Everything was so different, so exotic. He could hardly believe he was actually here.

Seeing it, hearing it, smelling it.

The group trekked on through the forest, following the winding path. They jumped narrow streams, climbed steep inclines, ducked under low branches.

The forest was constantly changing. Sometimes it closed in tight around them, with trees, lianas (climbing plants), flowering shrubs and soaring palms vying for space. In those areas, they were forced to stay on the path and it was impossible to see what was behind the thick curtains of greenery that surrounded them.

'Look at this,' Jake said, when they entered yet another part of the forest where everything was covered in brilliant green moss. He stopped by a fallen tree. The trunk was so long he couldn't see either end of it. But it wasn't the length that had caught his eye.

'What?' Sarah came back to see.

'All these ants.' Hundreds, maybe

thousands, of ants were swarming over the decaying trunk, running in and out of crevices in the bark. 'This is amazing.' Jake squatted down, trying to spot the entrance to their nest.

'Get a move on,' Sarah said. 'We don't want them having to send out a search party for us.'

They hurried after the rest of the group.

It was nearly six o'clock when they reached the camp. Jake flung his backpack down and gratefully accepted the cup of water he was offered. He sat on the grass to drink it. Sarah sat beside him. 'It's boiling, isn't it?' she said, downing her water in one thirsty gulp. 'So humid.'

Jake looked round the camp as he mopped his brow. It was set in a wide clearing, covered in dry, brown grass and dotted, here and there, with sawn-off tree stumps. Tents were clustered in the centre of the clearing. To one side, a huge, square, plastic water-tank rested on four rocks. On the opposite side of the camp, in a wide area of bare earth, a camp-fire burned brightly, sending up a column of grey smoke. A black cooking pot was suspended above it. All around the campsite, poles had been driven into the ground to hold lamps.

Jake could see groups of people sitting outside the tents, chatting and laughing together. A group of boys was playing football further off, dashing backwards and forwards after the ball. 'They must be mad,' Sarah said. 'Fancy running about in this heat.'

A Brazilian woman came to speak to the new arrivals.

'*Benvindo*. My name is Maria,' she said, smiling. 'I'm one of the organizers here. Welcome to High Tree Camp.' She pointed to a tree on the edge of the clearing. 'It's named after this kapok cotton tree, which is the tallest in this part of the forest. It was not felled by the Logan Corporation when they set up on this site because they are only interested in trees which fetch a high price on the world timber market.' She pointed to one of the tree stumps. 'You can see the damage they have done.'

'I hate them,' said Sarah to Jake in a whispered but determined tone.

Jake surveyed the kapok cotton tree. It was enormous. The trunk grew straight for 20 metres or more. A rope-like vine was twisted around it. Higher up, where the trunk divided into branches, a purple-flowered bush grew, its leafy stems stretching out along the tree's branches and hiding most of the tree's own canopy.

'The Logan Corporation abandoned this site, but they've restarted their operation in a new part of the forest, not far from here,' Maria went on. 'Now, with your help, we will drive them out *permanently*.'

'Good riddance,' Sarah said.

'Already, nearly two hundred people have joined us here,' Maria said, enthusiastically. She waved a hand around the camp. 'I'm sure you're all tired after your long journey so I won't delay you any longer. You can pitch your tents anywhere. Dinner will be ready at about eight o'clock and there will be a briefing for journalists at nine o'clock.' She smiled broadly. 'We're very grateful to you for coming so far to save the forest. There'll be a meeting at ten-thirty tomorrow morning to discuss details of the invasion.'

Jake frowned. The last thing he wanted to do was pitch his tent. It was too hot for anything energetic.

'One more thing,' Maria said, as the new arrivals began to disperse. 'August is the dry season here. Even so, we'd normally expect to get some rain. But this is an *El Nino* year so we haven't had rain for over a month. I expect you noticed how dry everything is.' A few people nodded. Maria went on: 'So we must be careful with our fires. One spark and the forest could be set alight.'

'What about the camp-fire, then?' Gill asked.

'We take great care with it. The area surrounding it has been cleared of anything that will burn. We put it out every night before going to sleep. And we never light a fire when there is a strong wind.'

Olly moved across to Jake.

'I suppose you've come to tell us what *El Nino* means,' Jake teased.

Olly scowled at him. 'It messes up the weather. I looked it up in my book.'

'It's a warm current off the coast of Peru,' Sarah said. 'We did it in geography last year. It comes every ten years or so and it disrupts the world's climate. Dry places get loads of rain. Wet places get droughts.'

'In my book –' Olly began.

'Where's Mum, Olly?' Jake asked, quickly. He was too tired to listen to Olly's amazing facts.

'She's talking to someone she used to work with. She said we should get our tent up and grab a space for hers.' Olly took Jake by the wrist and tried to pull him up. 'Come on. We've got to find a good place before everyone else nicks them all.'

Jake got reluctantly to his feet. Olly was right. They'd been on enough demos to know you had to find a tent-site quickly, otherwise you got left with the stony or sloping ground.

'How about over here?' Olly called over his shoulder as he sprinted across the clearing.

'See you later, Sarah,' Jake said, following his younger brother.

She nodded. 'Yeah. Hope you find a good pitch.'

Jake picked up his rucksack and trudged after Olly.

CHAPTER THREE

A log slipped in the camp-fire, sending sparks dancing into the air. Jake watched them contentedly; the sparks burned themselves out long before they touched the ground.

He wiped away a trickle of sweat from his forehead. He was so hot he felt as though he was frying. But you had to sit close to the fire if you didn't want to be bitten all over by mosquitoes.

His gaze travelled round the crowd of young people sitting near the camp-fire. There were Brazilians, Americans, Swedes, a couple of Germans and some more English people whose names Jake couldn't remember.

They were all laughing and joking.

'What other protests have you been on then, Jake?' Sarah asked. She was sitting next to him, her hair shining orange, reflecting the fire's flames.

He shrugged, trying to look nonchalant. 'I've been on loads of demos. I was at the nuclear-power protest in Aberwarey at Easter.'

'Were you?' She was clearly impressed. 'I was desperate to get to that but we had to go to Scotland for my cousin's wedding.' She pulled a face. 'I was one of the bridesmaids. Mind you, I managed to write some letters to government ministers complaining about their nuclear-power policy while we were there.'

'Did they reply?'

'Just the standard rubbish: *My comments had been noted.*' She shrugged. 'Tell me about Aberwarey. What was it like?'

'There were about four hundred of us and we . . .' Jake broke off, frowning. Olly was heading their way.

'I was at Framling Common last summer, though,' Sarah said. 'In Oxfordshire. Did you hear about that? A firm of property developers was going to cut down a row of trees so that people buying their houses would get a better view. In the end, they backed down and decided to leave the trees alone.'

'Result!' enthused Jake.

Olly arrived and threw himself down beside his elder brother. 'It's boiling,' he complained. He pulled off his T-shirt and wiped his face with it, leaving his blond hair standing up in damp spikes.

'That's because we're in Brazil,' Jake reminded him.

'Yeah, but it's even boiling for Brazil. I was talking to Diego, one of the first people to set up the camp, and he says it's not usually as hot as this. He reckons there's going to be a storm, even though it's the dry season.'

Jake laughed. There was nothing worse than a storm when you were camping. Somehow the rain always managed to find its way into your tent, soaking your sleeping-bag. And the next day the campsite would be thick with mud. There wouldn't be much chance of getting a good night's sleep either, with thunder booming all round and rain hammering on the tent.

Sarah smiled. 'We had a massive storm when I was protesting at Garnside Lake retail park. All our tents got washed away.'

'That happened to us when we were in

Aberwarey,' Olly said. 'Jake threw a wobbler because his Manchester United sleeping-bag got a teensy-weensy speck of mud on it.'

Jake glared at him. 'Brothers!' he said, defensively. 'They have such vivid imaginations when they're only eight years old.'

'You should have seen him when we were at Upper Meddingham for the wildlife demo,' Olly went on. 'He got up in the middle of the night to –'

'Isn't it past your bedtime?' Jake cut in, irritably.

Olly grinned. 'Mum said I could stay up till you went to bed.'

Jake's heart sank. He'd have a rotten time with Olly around. His brother had a knack for showing him up. 'Can't you find some other little kiddies to play with?' he demanded.

'I don't hang out with little kiddies. And anyway, it's too hot to do anything except sit around. And I keep getting bitten when I'm away from the fire.' He showed Jake the red lumps that were swelling on his arms.

'Well put your shirt back on then, and go and read a book in the tent.' Jake was determined to get rid of Olly somehow.

'And miss all the fun out here?' Olly leaned over Jake and dug Sarah in the ribs. 'Has he told you about the time he fell in the river when we were at Overingham?'

Sarah shook her head. She leaned forward, listening eagerly. Jake could see she was trying not to laugh.

'Nobody's interested in this, Olly,' Jake snapped.

'He was showing off, swinging across the river on a rope –'

'Shut up, Olly,' Jake cried, angrily.

Sarah winked at Olly. 'It sounds as though Jake gets up to all sorts of exciting things on your protests.'

Jake sighed. That was exactly the sort of encouragement Olly didn't need. He'd tell her every embarrassing incident he could think of now.

'When we went to Tritton last year, Jake made us miss the train because he couldn't find his boots,' Olly said. 'He had this huge row with Mum –'

'Belt up, Olly.'

'And you should have seen him at Bedlingbury Heath last October half-term. He –'

'I'm warning you –'

Olly ploughed on. '– he fell in this ditch and –'

Anger boiled up inside Jake. Couldn't Olly see that he'd gone too far? Jake didn't want everyone to know all the stupid things he'd done.

'– he got stuck in the mud. We had to get a rope. It took six people to pull him out.'

'Right!' Jake lunged at him. Olly gasped and ducked his thump. He scrambled to his feet and darted away from the fire. Jake pelted after him. 'Come back here,' he yelled.

Sarah started laughing. 'Leave it, Jake! He was only winding you up!'

'No way,' Jake shouted back. 'I'm going to kill him.'

Olly whimpered and kept going. He leaped over low tree stumps and zigzagged round taller ones.

Jake followed, running in and out of the pools of light cast by the lamps set on poles across the site. 'Come here, you little rat.'

Olly glanced round. His eyes were wide with fear and his mouth hung open, as he gasped for breath.

Jake stopped running. His brother had learned his lesson. With any luck, he'd go to bed now and leave Jake to get to know Sarah some more.

He watched Olly keep running. He wasn't

heading for the tents. He was almost out of range of the camp lights now, running towards the edge of the clearing – towards the rain forest.

Jake frowned. Surely Olly wouldn't be stupid enough to venture in there. Not after all the warnings they'd had. 'Come back, you idiot,' he called. He pulled his torch out of his pocket and switched it on, spotlighting his brother. Against the towering trees ahead, Olly looked tiny.

Olly kept on running.

Jake's heart began to pound. 'Stop, Olly! Don't go into the forest.'

But Olly didn't stop. He reached the edge of the clearing and plunged into the forest.

Jake pelted after him. 'For Pete's sake, Olly, you know we're not supposed to go in there.'

There was no answer.

Jake stopped on the brink of the forest. He shone his torch in among the trees. 'Olly,' he called. 'Come out of there!' He was sure Olly hadn't gone far. He was probably hiding behind the first tree, trying to make Jake feel guilty for chasing him. 'Olly, don't be an idiot!'

There was still no reply.

He could hear rustling in the undergrowth

and groaned. Olly really had gone into the forest. Typical! And now Jake would have to go after him and bring him back. Still, if he listened carefully he'd be able to follow Olly, and with his longer legs, he'd soon catch up with him. In a couple of minutes they'd both be safely back in the camp.

Jake stepped in among the trees.

CHAPTER FOUR

The forest seemed to close in around Jake as soon as he left the camp clearing. He swung his torch around but, after the brightness of the camp lights, its beam seemed feeble. He could see pale creepers and tangles of glossy-leaved bushes. But there were too many hollows of blackness that the torch couldn't illuminate for Jake's liking.

'Where are you, Olly?' Jake called.

He took a tentative next step forward.

There was no reply.

Jake strained his ears, listening for Olly's movements. He heard a swishing noise ahead of him, as though someone was pushing through the undergrowth. He moved towards it. 'Come back, Olly. It's dangerous out here.'

Olly still didn't reply and Jake could feel fear growing inside him. Anything could happen to them out here, in the dark. He pushed the thought away and felt anger flood through him. He wanted to sit by the camp-fire with the other teenagers, not go traipsing through the forest trying to find his kid brother. Especially in this heat.

'Olly,' he called again, more sharply this time. 'Where are you?'

'Jake.' Olly's voice quavered. 'I think I'm lost.'

He sounds quite a way ahead, Jake thought as he came upon a path that led in what he hoped was the right direction and hurried along it. 'Stand still and keep talking so I can find you,' he called out.

'I want Mum,' Olly wailed.

Jake could hear him moving again. Or maybe it wasn't him. Maybe it was some animal. He stopped. He didn't want to go the wrong way. 'Are you standing still, Olly?'

'I'm looking for you.'

'I told you to stand still.' Jake couldn't believe Olly's stupidity. 'How can you expect me to find you if you keep wandering about?'

He wiped away trickles of sweat from his face and went on, moving as quickly as he could through the dense undergrowth. 'Keep talking. I'll follow the sound of your voice.'

Wings fluttered above Jake's head. He ducked instinctively as something flashed past him and disappeared among the trees. It was just a bird, he told himself. But he was getting rattled.

'Olly!' he yelled. 'Where are you?'

There was a scuffling sound to his right. Something let out a long, piercing shriek. Jake jumped. What was there? The bushes were swaying but there was nothing else to be seen. He went on again, trying not to look at the bugs that scurried for cover when the torch swept over them on the rain forest floor. By day, Jake would have been fascinated by them. But now, in the darkness, he kept remembering that spider Olly had talked about – the Brazilian wandering spider – the deadliest spider in the world. Perhaps there were dozens of them lurking under leaves, waiting for a chance to bite anyone who came too close.

'Where are you, Jake?'

Jake turned in the direction of Olly's voice. 'I'm looking for you!' He left the path, trying to memorize the route he was taking so they could get back to the camp again.

A sudden flash of lightning illuminated the forest for an instant.

It was followed by a long, low rumble of thunder.

'J–Jake.' Olly sounded terrified.

'It's all right,' Jake said. 'It's only thunder. It won't hurt you.' Olly had always been scared of storms, especially when they came at night. 'Have you got your torch?'

'Yes.'

'Switch it on then. It'll make you feel better.'

'It is switched on.'

Jake's heart missed a beat. All Jake could see was darkness. He moved forward again. There was a second flash of lightning and more thunder, louder this time.

'Be quick, Jake. I don't like it.'

A glimmer of light caught Jake's eye. At last! Olly's torch! Sighing with relief, Jake headed for the light, stumbling over the uneven ground.

He found Olly huddled against a tree. He was crying. 'Jake, I didn't know where you were.'

'Don't worry – I'm here now.' Jake bit back

the urge to snap at his brother. They wouldn't be out here if Olly hadn't run off – but there was no point making things worse. He put his arm round Olly's heaving shoulders. 'Come on, we've got to get back to the camp.'

He led Olly back the way he'd come. They soon reached the path and Jake turned right along it. 'Won't be long now.'

'Are we going the right way?' Olly asked, when they'd been walking for about ten minutes. 'I thought we should have turned back there.'

Jake shone his torch round uncertainly. 'Are you sure?'

'No. But we seem to have been going a long time.'

Jake hesitated. He wasn't sure. Maybe Olly was right. They retraced their steps, looking out for the camp lights. But the forest was dense and, even when they switched their torches off, there seemed to be nothing but darkness in all directions.

After another few minutes of walking, Jake stopped. He looked round, grimly. They were well and truly lost.

The storm was getting closer. There was no gap now between the lightning and the thunder. Flash. Boom. Flash. Boom. But there was still no rain and the temperature seemed to be rising, despite the fact that a light breeze had sprung up. Leaves, stirred by the wind, rippled and trembled all around them.

'I'm hot,' Olly complained. 'And I'm tired.'

'Me too,' Jake said. 'But we'll have to put up with it.' Another path crossed theirs. Jake shone the torch along it in both directions. 'Which way now?'

'Down here, I think,' Olly said, pointing left. They turned and trudged on in silence.

'Perhaps we should shout,' Jake suggested, at last. 'Someone in the camp might hear us.' He was beginning to realize their task was hopeless. For all he knew, they could be walking round in circles.

They waited for a clap of thunder to die away. 'Help! We're lost! Can anybody hear us?'

Thunder rolled again, drowning their voices. In the few seconds of quiet that followed it, they listened intently. No answering cry. Nothing but the night sounds of the forest. There was another crash of thunder, so loud this time that Olly clung to Jake.

'Shout again,' Jake cried, as it faded to a low rumble.

They yelled together. 'Help! We're lost! Help!'

It was useless. Nobody answered their shouts.

'If we don't find the camp now, we'll find it in the morning, when it gets light, won't we, Jake?' Olly asked. He started to cough.

Jake slapped him on the back. 'Of course we will. And when you get back to school, you'll be able to tell everyone about how you got lost in a Brazilian rain forest.'

Olly groaned. 'No, I won't. Everyone says my new teacher, Miss Clark, makes you write about exciting stuff you've done. But I'm going to say I watched videos every day.'

Jake laughed and ruffled his brother's hair. 'We ought to get a move on.'

They set off again.

'There! What's that?' Olly asked.

Jake looked up. There was an orange glow ahead. 'The camp-fire!' he cried as a sense of relief flooded through him. They headed towards it, hurrying now that they knew where they were going.

All around them the forest was alive with movement. Small animals and insects were scurrying past them. Now that his fear of being lost had subsided, Jake half wished he could stop and take a closer look at them. But he could see that Olly was worn out.

Jake held his brother's hand. He guided Olly forward, keeping a wary eye out for snakes.

'I suppose Mum'll tell us off,' Olly said gloomily.

'Bound to,' Jake said. But he didn't care. He was just glad they'd found their way back at last. A black and cream mottled snake wriggled out from under a bush ahead of them. Jake tensed and instinctively jerked Olly out of its way. It was followed by hordes of scurrying beetles. Olly swung his torch beam up into the tree branches. 'Look at all those monkeys. They're having a race.'

Jake watched uneasily. Every living creature seemed to be heading in one direction.

The opposite direction to the one they were taking.

Jake shrugged. Perhaps it was always like this at night. Perhaps they were all heading for a pool to get a drink. His eyes began to water. He wiped them with the back of his hand. 'Come on.' He'd be glad to get back. A cough tickled the back of his throat.

They went on. 'I can smell the smoke now,' Olly said. 'We'll be back soon.' He coughed as if to prove his point.

Jake sniffed the heavy air a couple of times. He could smell smoke too, quite distinctly. And the orange glow ahead seemed to be spreading out.

It was much too wide to be the camp-fire.

Jake stopped and yanked on Olly's arm. 'Wait!'

The hair on the back of Jake's neck prickled.

'Ow!' cried Olly. 'What's up?'

Jake trembled. Now he understood why all the animals and insects were going the other way. And he realized, too, why they were both coughing all of a sudden. 'That's not the camp-fire, Olly,' he cried. 'It's a forest fire.'

CHAPTER FIVE

The forest was on fire.

The crackling spread of the bright orange flames whispered through the trees towards them.

Jake's heart skipped a beat.

'What are we going to do?' Olly asked, fearfully. He tugged anxiously on Jake's arm and shuffled his feet.

Jake struggled to stay calm. 'I don't know.' His head pounded with such fear that he could hardly think straight. His instinct was to run. Maria had said the forest was dry so the fire would spread rapidly, but where should they run to? They couldn't find the camp and if they simply raced off into the forest they might go the wrong way and get trapped by the fire.

Then he remembered the forest creatures. They knew what to do. 'We've got to follow the animals.'

They turned and ran. Jake kept a tight hold on Olly's hand, frightened of them becoming separated again. The acrid smell of burning was everywhere and smoke hung thickly beneath the forest canopy. It was seeping between the trees almost as fast as they could run. Their eyes streamed and they were coughing hard.

Several minutes later the air became clearer. It was still humid and heavy, but there was no smoke.

At last Jake halted. He loosened his grip on Olly's hand.

'What's wrong? Why are we stopping?'

'I think the fire's going the other way.' Jake shone his torch along the path ahead. The forest creatures' frenzied dash for safety was over. The sounds of the night were back.

When Jake swung the torch beam up into the branches above them, he could see bats swooping between the trees in their search for food. The sight was reassuring: if the animals were behaving normally again, then the danger must have passed.

Relief coursed through him. The situation was still serious but at least he and Olly were in no immediate danger. They had time to think. And plan. Jake looked back the way they'd come. A few wisps of smoke hung in the air, like grey ghosts in the torchlight. But there was no sign of any flames.

'How did the fire start?' Olly asked, rasping for breath.

'This way,' said Jake, tugging Olly back along the path in search of their camp again. 'The lightning probably started it.' Jake shrugged. 'Maybe it struck a tree. We'll tell Maria about it when we get back. She'll know what   to do.' He yawned, suddenly overcome with weariness.

Olly yawned too. 'I want to go to bed,' he said.

'We'll find the camp in a minute,' Jake said, trying to reassure him.

The path forked and they followed the left branch. Before long, though, it became impassable with dense overhanging leaves and rutted earth. 'We'll have to go back,' Jake said, despondently. He was fed up with trudging around, not knowing where they were going.

Olly groaned. 'I'm tired, Jake.'

'I know. We're both tired. But you want to find the camp, don't you?'

'We can find it in the morning.' Olly flung himself down on the ground. 'Let's sleep here.'

Jake thought it over. He didn't fancy spending the night in the forest: any one of the dangerous creatures Olly kept going on about could creep up on them while they slept. But there wasn't much point in traipsing on and on, trying to get back to camp. For all they knew, they could already be going in the wrong direction entirely. They could end up miles away. And they were both desperately tired. The long journey and the heat had worn them out.

He crouched down beside Olly. 'Perhaps we should stop here. We could take it in turns to keep watch. What d'you think?'

There was no reply.

Jake shone the torch on his brother. He was already fast asleep.

Jake smiled. Olly had always been able to sleep in odd situations. There was a photo of him in an album at home that showed him dozing in his high chair with a sandwich in one hand. He'd nodded off in a shoe shop once, too, when they had been buying a new pair of trainers for Jake.

Jake sat down. He switched off Olly's torch but he kept his own turned on. He wouldn't sleep, he decided. He'd sit here watching and listening in case of danger.

It wasn't long, though, before his head began to nod. He sat up straighter, trying to stay awake. But his eyelids felt heavy. They kept on shutting, no matter how hard he battled to keep them open. In the end, his head fell forward on to his knees and he slept.

It was already light when Jake woke up. He opened his eyes and found himself lying on the forest floor, on a bed of long grass, looking up at huge trees searching for the sky.

The memories of last night's events flooded back to him with a jolt and he groaned.

Olly was still asleep, lying stretched out on one side with his arm curled under his head. Jake shook him. 'Wake up, Olly.'

Olly stirred. 'Whassat?'

'We've got to get back to our camp. Mum'll be going frantic.' Jake stood up and stretched. He was surprised to find that there was still smoke in the air.

Olly stood up too. His clothes were

crumpled and there was a small black and orange beetle clinging to his shoulder. Jake knocked it off.

'How are we going to find the camp?' Olly asked, sleepily.

'We'll follow this path and hope we spot something we recognize,' Jake said, with more confidence than he felt. He set off, with Olly trailing behind him.

'Do you think the fire's really gone out?' Olly asked.

'It must have burned itself out last night,' Jake said. 'These last few wisps of smoke are all that are left of it.' He flapped his hand, dispersing the smoke that was within range.

'But they sometimes burn for months,' Olly said. 'And huge bits of forest get burned up.'

'Not this time. This fire went out last night.' Jake spoke firmly. He desperately wanted to believe himself and didn't want to consider the possibility that the fire could still be alight.

They walked on in silence for a while. A flock of red birds flew by and they caught a glimpse of a gaudy parrot, brilliant against the dark leaves overhead.

'We need to find that big tree on the edge

of the campsite,' Olly said, when they'd been walking for about twenty minutes. 'If we could see that, we'd know where to go.'

Jake halted. 'That's it, Olly! You're a genius!'

'Am I?'

'You've cracked it! If I climb a tree, I'll be able to look across the top of the forest and spot the tree by our camp.'

Olly grabbed Jake's hand. 'You can't. Those trees are miles high. What if you fall?'

Jake shook him off. 'I won't fall. I've climbed loads of trees.'

'Not as high as these.'

'I'll be OK.' Jake glanced at the thick tree trunks around them. 'This one looks good.' The tree was crooked, with plenty of branches, and there were vines wrapped all the way up it to give hand- and footholds. Jake pulled himself into it and started to climb.

'Stay there,' he shouted back over his shoulder after he had pulled himself up the first couple of metres. 'You can catch me if I fall.'

'Be careful,' said Olly.

After a spell of energetic climbing, Jake paused and looked down. The ground was about ten metres below. It looked a disconcertingly long way. Olly was gazing up at him and, even from this height, Jake could see the worried expression on his face. 'Don't worry, Olly, I won't fall.'

Jake looked up. The remainder of the tree seemed to stretch on for ever. He swallowed hard, suddenly unnerved by the thought of going so high.

'What's up?' Olly called up.

'Nothing.' Jake tried to sound unperturbed. 'I'm just getting my breath back.' He moved up again.

Now the climb became more difficult. For one thing, the branches were becoming thinner. They swayed under his weight. There were leaves here, too, and he had to push through them as he climbed. But it was the height of the tree that made things hardest. He'd climbed plenty of trees before but he'd never been as high as this. The thought of the long drop to the ground was daunting.

He paused for a breather and looked around, peering through the leaves, holding tight to a branch. He half expected to see monkeys staring at him but the only creatures visible were the ants that swarmed busily along the branches, and a pair of turquoise birds that watched him from a safe distance.

He went on again, banishing all thoughts of danger. He'd made up his mind to get to the top of this tree and now he was going to do it.

The light grew stronger as Jake climbed and suddenly his head emerged into brilliant sunlight. The sky was bright blue and cloudless. The air was still. He pulled himself a little higher and looked around.

He was surrounded by an undulating patchwork of varied greens, stretching for as far as he could see like puffy clouds. Further off, the river glittered in the sunlight. The beauty of the scene swept away Jake's anxiety. It was stunning.

Then he spotted the tall kapok tree that he knew stood on the edge of High Tree Camp. It was to his right, not far away, and it was enormous – easily 20 metres taller than the other trees surrounding it. Jake was about to climb down again when he noticed something else. He narrowed his eyes, trying to see more clearly. It was moving beyond the tall tree, dancing across the leafy canopy, flickering, stretching tall then shrinking back. Above it, the sky was strangely dark. And suddenly Jake knew what it was.

The forest fire was still burning.

CHAPTER SIX

Jake's mind was racing as he climbed down the tree. There was no wind but the fire looked as though it was close to the camp. He could imagine it creeping through the forest, spreading out, putting all the protesters in danger. He thought of Mum, of Sarah and of all the others they'd met. He and Olly had to warn them. Heedless now of the height of the tree, Jake scrambled down, swiftly lowering himself from branch to branch.

As he emerged from the leaves, Olly's voice reached him: 'Could you see it?'

'Yes. I'll tell you when I get down.'

A couple of metres from the ground, Jake jumped. He landed on his feet. 'Quick, Olly!'

he cried. 'Follow me!' He set off running into the trees in the direction of the camp. 'The fire's got going again. It's heading straight for the camp.' He didn't look back but he could hear his brother's footsteps pounding along behind him.

They charged along the narrow path, jumping over small fallen branches and wayward bushes. The smoke was thicker now and, in the occasional shafts of sunlight that reached to the forest floor, they could see it curling and writhing. It made them cough, and soon forced them to slow down.

The path turned sharp right, away from the tall kapok tree.

'This way,' Jake cried. He left the path and plunged into the forest. They dodged in and out, always heading in the direction of the camp.

Soon they could hear the fire, cracking and hissing. They could smell the same sharp, acrid smell of burning plant life that they'd noticed last night, too.

Suddenly Jake stopped. Olly barged into his back. 'Oomph,' he let out. 'What now?' he demanded.

Jake didn't answer. He simply stared ahead, transfixed by horror. They'd almost reached the camp now. He could see the clearing through the trees and the network of tents.

'What is it?' Olly cried. He tried to push past Jake.

Jake held him back. 'The camp's on fire.'

'What about Mum?'

Flames were ripping through the tents.

Jake could feel the heat of the flames stroke his cheeks. He put a restraining arm across to bar Olly's continued attempts to go closer. 'No. Stay back.'

The camp was deserted. There were no cries for help nor any other movement or signs of life. 'They must have heard the fire coming and run off,' Jake said. 'Mum'll be OK. She'll have escaped.'

'What are we going to do, Jake?' Olly trembled and edged a few unconscious steps backwards.

'I don't know.' Jake shivered, in spite of the heat.

The flames spread out from tent to tent, running across the dry grass. The smoke was becoming more dense. They coughed and tried to blink away the irritation from their streaming eyes. All Jake could think about was that he and Olly were by themselves. As the oldest, it was up to him to keep Olly safe. But how was he going to do it?

'Let's just get out of here!' Jake grabbed Olly's hand and ran with him, away from the fire. They blundered through the under-growth, slapping higher branches aside as low bushes whipped their legs. The noise of the fire lessened as they ran but Jake knew it was advancing after them all the same. They'd got to keep running. But where should they run to? Maria had told them how dry the forest was. Nowhere would be safe. Except . . .

'The river!' Jake cried. 'We've got to get to the river. We'll find the loggers' road and follow that. It leads all the way there.' He glanced back in the direction of the camp, trying to get his bearings. 'This way.' He steered Olly to the left.

Before long, they came upon a narrow path. It seemed to be heading in the right direction. They ran down it and suddenly they were out of the forest. The road, bright with sunlight, stretched away into the distance. There was no sign of the other protesters but Jake guessed they were somewhere ahead. If they could catch up with them, they'd find out for sure if Mum was OK.

They raced along the road. The air was fresher here and, with no obstacles blocking their way, they made good progress. Jake looked back as they ran. He could still see the orange light of the flames between the trees but with no wind it was moving slowly.

'What's that?' Olly asked, pointing ahead.

In the distance, a yellow vehicle was crawling across the road in front of them. It stopped on the edge of the forest to the left of the road. 'I don't know,' Jake said.

'Maybe it's a fire engine, or something,' suggested Olly.

'Doubt it,' answered Jake.

A figure darted away from the vehicle and disappeared into the forest on the opposite side of the road.

As they drew nearer, a second vehicle appeared. It crossed the road too and stopped beside the first one.

'It looks like a bulldozer.' Jake frowned. Who would be driving bulldozers around with a fire raging?

'Perhaps they're trying to make a fire-break,' Olly suggested. 'I read about it at school. When there's a forest fire, people uproot a whole load of trees and bushes so the fire hasn't got anything to burn.'

Jake looked back at the fire. They were quite a way ahead of it now. 'We could give them a hand. We did come here to save the forest, after all.'

Olly darted ahead. 'I hope they let me drive one of those bulldozers!'

There was nobody by the bulldozers when they reached them but Jake spotted a clearing, to the west of the road, with another, narrower road leading into it. 'Over here, Olly,' he said.

They went into the clearing. It was a wide area, four or five times the size of the protesters' camp. The ground was scarred with tree stumps. Wooden huts stood in the centre of the clearing. A tractor and a forklift truck were parked next to them. Beyond them were more huts and a stack of logs arranged, one on top of the other, in a tidy pile. They were held in place by wooden stakes that had been driven into the ground.

On the far side, an open-air kitchen stood beside a water-tank. A trestle table was set up here. One of the long benches that served as seating was tipped over. 'Looks like somebody left in a hurry,' Olly said.

'This must be the loggers' camp,' Jake said.

'Hey!' The voice made both boys jump.

They spun round. Sarah was hurrying towards them. 'Thank goodness you're all right. Everyone was really worried about you two.'

Jake gawped at her. 'What are you doing here?'

'I'm making sure all the loggers' equipment gets destroyed in the fire.' She brushed away some dirt from her cheek.

Jake was astonished. 'Are you mad?'

'The fire's scared the loggers off,' Sarah said, defiantly. 'But as soon as it burns itself out, they'll come back and start cutting down trees again.'

'The fire will burn all their equipment anyway.'

She shook her head. 'The fire's the wrong side of the road. It'll act as a fire-break. Everything on this side of the road will be untouched.'

'So you're driving all their machines across the road.'

Sarah nodded. 'It's not hard when you get the hang of it. In fact, the only difficult thing was sneaking off without my parents noticing.'

'Has everyone else gone to the river?' Jake asked.

'Yes.'

'What about Mum?' Olly asked.

Sarah hesitated for a moment. 'I'm sure she did,' she said, frowning at Jake. 'Everyone got out of our camp. There was a terrible panic because it was so early. Most people were still in bed.'

'Go and get yourself a drink, Olly,' Jake said. 'I expect you're thirsty after all this time. And see if you can find anything to eat.' He suspected Sarah was lying and he wanted to speak to her without Olly overhearing.

Olly headed for the water-tank.

'Mum didn't go to the river, did she?' Jake said. 'You only told Olly that so he wouldn't get upset.'

Sarah looked down at her boots. 'She went off into the forest, last night, to look for you two.'

Jake glanced back the way they'd come. Mum was out there somewhere. He shivered, remembering the way the flames had streaked across the camp.

'Paulo went with her.' Sarah rested a hand on Jake's arm. 'He knows the forest. She'll be all right with him.'

Jake nodded. It was comforting to know that she wasn't alone but she was still in danger. He moved to the edge of the clearing and peered in among the trees, hoping somehow to spot her but knowing he wouldn't.

The forest was choked with smoke and he could hear the crackle of burning wood, too. Suddenly, he spotted a flicker of orange light. 'The fire's coming!' he yelled. 'It's coming this way!'

A tapir, a bulky, grey animal with a pointed snout, came blundering out of the forest. It was nearly a metre tall. Jake jumped aside and watched as it careered across the clearing. Behind it came other creatures too: rats, some of them nearly half a metre long; a couple of armadillos, running one behind the other; scores of insects – huge cockroaches, beetles, ants, a giant black and orange centipede. Jake's heart sank. He'd come to Brazil hoping to see creatures like these. But not when they were running scared.

'How did the fire get across the road?' Sarah sounded bewildered.

'I don't know. Unless . . .' Perhaps the fire hadn't crossed the road. The road ended at the protesters' camp. The fire must have spread through the trees beyond it and now it was coming down both sides of the road. Jake darted into the centre of the clearing, calling for Olly. Sarah followed him.

Olly came running clutching an armful of oranges and with a half-eaten banana chunk sticking out of his mouth.

'We've got to get out,' Jake cried urgently. Olly dropped the oranges. 'The fire's heading this way.'

CHAPTER SEVEN

Jake, Olly and Sarah raced out of the clearing and emerged on to the road near the abandoned bulldozers. A light breeze had sprung up. It was coming from behind them. Jake's stomach tightened. The fire would travel more quickly with a wind driving it.

Smoke wafted along the road. To their left, the breeze had pushed the flames ahead of them. They hadn't reached the road yet, but they were plainly visible between the trees. The children could feel the heat of the fire, too, and hear it eating its way through the forest.

'We've got to get in front of it,' Jake cried.

'Otherwise it could block our way to the river.'

They ran, sticking to the right side of the road. The fire on that side was still behind them and the heat was less intense there. To their left, though, the fire was raging. Trees and bushes at the roadside ahead were starting to burn and topple. Fire licked up vines and spread into the canopies overhead. Burning leafy debris rained down.

'We'll have to get off the road!' Sarah cried. She plunged into the forest. Jake and Olly followed her.

The rain forest was alive with fleeing wildlife. Screeching monkeys swung from tree to tree. Flocks of brilliantly coloured birds skimmed overhead. Jake looked out for snakes as he ran. They'd be on the move too, and he didn't want to run into one.

'The river's south of here, I think,' he said. 'If we stay close to the road we won't get lost.'

The forest became more dense. Tall palms and tree ferns were packed tightly together with hardly any space between their trunks. Vines thicker than a man's arm hung down. The forest floor was hidden by young trees and by smaller ferns. They went on in silence, concentrating on every step. But they were moving painfully slowly for fear of tripping up and the density of the forest was gradually forcing them away from the road. Jake urged and pushed Olly on ahead of him, where he could see him. His brother was drained. They all were.

Jake looked back. He couldn't see the flames but he could hear the crack of burning wood and he knew the fire was gaining on them. The smoke was getting thicker too. Breathing it in hurt his nose and throat. His eyes were still streaming and they were all coughing hard.

Fear churned inside him. His brain was commanding him to run, to get away from the fire before it trapped him. But he couldn't run. There was no space to run. All they could do was keep on battling through the undergrowth.

At last the trees began to thin out a little. Now they were tall and narrow, with no low-hanging branches. The ground was covered in dry, brown leaves and a tangle of low-growing plants. Jake's hopes soared. They could go faster here.

'This is better,' Sarah cried. 'We've got a chance of outrunning the fire if it's like this all the way to the river.' They raced through the trees, glad to be moving quickly again. Though they couldn't see the road, they knew they were heading in the right direction because forest creatures were streaming along with them. Jake knew animals followed their instinct to escape danger and the thought was reassuring.

When the forest began to close in again, they stopped for a moment to get their breath back. Jake looked behind him. The flames were visible now, licking along the edge of the densely-packed forest they'd left only a few minutes before. Jake's heart seemed to leap into his throat. The fire was spreading rapidly into the open area they'd just crossed. Sparks from the burning trees were raining down, setting dead leaves alight.

'There's a path here,' Sarah said. Now Sarah pushed Olly ahead of her. Jake followed them. He heard Olly scream. Then there was a thud.

'What's happened?' Jake cried, trying to see past Sarah.

'He's fallen in a hole.' Sarah sounded shocked. 'It had leaves and twigs over it. It looked just like the path until he stepped on it.'

Jake squeezed past her. Olly was lying in the bottom of a pit. Miraculously, his glasses had stayed on. He looked frighteningly pale. Jake crouched down. 'Are you OK?'

'My ankle hurts.' Olly winced as he tried to move it.

The pit was about two metres deep. Its bottom was strewn with thin branches and leaves. An animal trap, Jake thought. 'Can you get up?' he asked. 'We'll pull you out.'

Olly started to stand up, then he sank down, clutching his ankle and groaning. 'It hurts.'

'Come on, Olly.' Jake tried to still the quaver of fear in his voice. 'We've got to get you out of there. The fire's coming.'

'I can't. I can't.' He was crying.

Jake looked back. Flames were running across the fallen leaves behind them and streaking up into the trees. He guessed they were no more than 30 metres away.

'You've *got* to stand up,' Jake shouted into the hole. 'If you stay in there, the fire will get all of us.'

Olly sobbed harder than ever. 'It hurts too much.'

'Come on, Olly,' Sarah said, encouragingly. 'Try and stand on one leg.'

Sparks showered around them.

Jake threw himself down on his stomach and leaned over the edge of the pit, stretching out with both arms. 'Stand up and get hold of my hands. I'll pull you out.'

More sparks rained down. Some of them fell into the pit. Olly's eyes widened with fear. 'The fire's in here with me!'

'That's why you've got to get out,' Jake yelled.

A flame appeared in a pile of leaves on the far side of the pit.

Sobbing with pain, Olly stumbled to his feet. 'Help, Jake.'

'Come over here and stretch your arms up to me.'

Olly cowered against the far side of the pit, staring at the flame, transfixed with terror. A second flame appeared. It licked along a twig. 'It'll burn me,' Olly whimpered.

'For God's sake, Olly.' Jake wrenched off his T-shirt. It was damp with sweat. He hurled it at the flames, praying that it would smother them. The T-shirt missed. It flopped down beside the fire. The flames grew higher. They were spreading to the twigs and leaves that littered the bottom of the pit.

'Come over here,' Jake cried. He leaned into the pit as far as he dared. 'Hang on to my belt, Sarah.'

He felt his belt tighten and he knew she

was holding him. He wriggled further forward, stretching out to Olly.

A spark landed in among the leaves of a tree fern only a couple of metres away. It glowed brightly, then a tiny flame flicked out. It began to inch along a wide, brown leaf, multiplying as it went. The noise and heat of the fire was growing by the second. There wasn't much time left.

At last the urgency of the situation seemed to get through to Olly. He took two hurried, limping steps across the pit and reached up to Jake. Jake caught his hands. 'I've got him!' he yelled. 'Pull me back.'

With Sarah wrenching on his belt, Jake hauled Olly out of the pit. Olly cried out in pain and then sank down on the ground, clutching his injured ankle.

The fire was close behind them now. Jake could feel it scorching his bare skin. It roared like a wild animal. He didn't want to look at it but he couldn't stop himself from turning to see how near it was.

His stomach lurched. Behind him was a living wall of fire. Hissing, crackling flames licked around tree trunks and soared high into the leafy canopies. There was smoke everywhere and the heat was unbearable.

'Run, Sarah!' Jake yelled. He scooped Olly up in his arms. Gasping for air, he stumbled away from the fire, skirting round the pit. Smoke filled his lungs as he set off along the path. He coughed violently and the smoke meant he could barely see where he was going. He blundered on, staggering under Olly's weight.

Olly clung to his neck. He was coughing too. His body jerked with the effort. 'It's going to catch us,' he croaked.

'No it isn't.' Jake wasn't giving in, though his arms felt ready to drop off. He glanced back over his shoulder. The gap between them and the fire was wider now.

They could still outrun it.

There was still a chance they'd survive.

CHAPTER EIGHT

Olly was heavy. 'I'll have to put you down for a minute,' Jake panted. He lowered his brother to the ground and stood, hunched over, trying to get his breath back.

'My turn, Jake. I'll give him a piggyback,' Sarah said. She bent down so Olly could clamber on to her back.

'Cheers.' Jake clutched his side and breathed deeply as he tried to rid himself of a nagging stitch.

They set off again, their senses alert for signs that the fire was catching up with them. But, though the forest was becoming more dense, the path was relatively clear and they seemed to be leaving the fire behind again.

Suddenly they heard a crashing sound behind them. Whirling round they saw a grey, bristly, wild pig charging towards them. They threw themselves out of its way as it hurtled past, brushing their legs. A moment later, more pigs burst out of the undergrowth, squealing and grunting.

'Do you think there are any more of them?' Sarah asked, shakily, when they'd disappeared into the undergrowth on the other side.

'I hope not,' Jake said. 'That was a bit close for comfort.' He wiped his clammy hands on his shorts.

'What were they?' Olly sounded shocked.

'Peccaries,' Jake said. He laughed wryly. 'When we were planning this trip, I hoped I might see one.'

They went on but, before long, the path veered to the right. 'It looks as though it's going the wrong way for the river,' Jake said, uncertainly.

'It might turn again further on and get us back on track,' Sarah replied.

Jake frowned. 'It might lead us towards the fire, too.' The insects that had been scurrying along with them were leaving the path and disappearing into the forest. 'We ought to follow the forest creatures.'

'They're smaller than us,' Sarah pointed out. 'They can get underneath bushes. We've got to find a way round them.'

Jake stepped off the path. The forest ahead was heavily overgrown but maybe they could force their way through. 'We've got to keep heading south,' he said. 'Otherwise we might not find our way to the river.' The authorities in Manaus must have spotted the smoke by now and they were sure to have sent rescue boats.

'But what about . . .?' Sarah began.

'If we head south we know we'll come to the river eventually,' Jake said, trying to convince her. He looked back the way they'd come. He couldn't see the fire yet but the noise of the flames was growing.

'Yes, but . . .' Sarah sounded annoyed.

'It's too risky to stay on the path,' Jake said. He hoped they weren't going to have a row. They'd got enough to worry about without falling out over the best route to take.

'Cut it out, you two,' said Olly as he clung to Sarah's shoulders.

Sarah must have felt the same because she ducked into the forest. 'Lead the way, then,' she said.

It wasn't easy to get through the forest.

Gaps between the trees were almost non-existent. In places, their trunks were actually touching and the trio had to make long detours to get past. Vines were a problem too. They hung from the branches in tight clusters. Some of them had rooted themselves in the ground, effectively closing off escape routes.

Jake and Sarah talked as they went along, trying to take their minds off the danger. They stuck to neutral subjects – music, school mates and favourite TV programmes – anything that didn't remind them of fire.

At last they were brought to a standstill by a wall of impenetrable forest. Dismayed, they moved to their right, looking for a way through. It seemed an age before Jake spotted a small gap beneath the spiny stems of a glossy-leaved shrub.

'Here. Through here.' He lifted Olly down from Sarah's back. 'We'll have to crawl.'

Sarah went first, followed by Olly. He didn't complain but it was evident that his ankle was painful. He dragged it behind him as he inched his way under the bush. Jake wondered if it was broken. He felt a wave of sympathy for Olly. No wonder he was so quiet. He must be in agony.

When it was Jake's turn to go through the low gap, he kept his head down to guard his eyes from the sharp thorns. He came out on the other side. Olly was sitting on the ground, white-faced, nursing his ankle. Sarah was gazing round in dismay. 'There's no way through from here,' she said, desperately.

Jake scanned the undergrowth. There had to be a way out. They didn't have time to retrace their steps. So far, the fire had been moving slowly enough for them to outrun it but any hold-ups gave it the chance to catch up with them again.

'We can get through there,' Olly said, suddenly. He pointed to a narrow space between two trees. Jake stared. He wasn't sure that it was wide enough. 'It's lucky I play so much basketball,' he said, trying to lighten the air of gloom that had settled on them. 'I'd never fit through there if I was any fatter.'

Olly stood up awkwardly. He balanced on one foot for a moment, then limped to the opening, wincing at every step. He disappeared through the opening. Sarah turned sideways, breathing in and making herself as thin as possible. 'Wish me luck,' she said. She squeezed through after him.

Then it was Jake's turn. The rough bark

tore his bare skin as he forced his way through, but he bit his lip and kept going. The gap was frighteningly narrow. His chest was so compressed, he could barely breathe. His back scraped along the trunk. Panic coursed through him. He might get stuck. He might have to stay there, wedged between the trunks, until the fire got him. He struggled furiously. He had to get through. *He had to.*

A brilliant yellow snake dropped down above Jake's head, its tail looped round a branch. Its head hung level with Jake's face. The lidless eyes peered at Jake. Its tongue flicked in and out.

Jake froze. He stared at the snake, wide-eyed with horror, terrified that it might suddenly lunge at him. He'd seen one like it in Olly's book. He was pretty sure it was a golden eyelash viper – one of the most poisonous creatures in the forest.

The snake hung motionless, for a moment. Then it arched towards Jake, lifting its head. Jake's heart pounded violently. Sweat trickled down his face.

The snake drew closer. Its body touched Jake's shoulder. It felt cold, smooth and deadly. A scream welled up in Jake's throat. He pressed his lips tightly together, forcing himself to stay silent. A sudden sound might startle the snake into attacking.

The snake released its grip on the branch and coiled itself round Jake's arm. Then, slowly, it slithered down to the ground and disappeared into the forest.

A wave of nausea swept over Jake. His hands shook uncontrollably as he battled to get out from between the two trees.

'What's keeping you?' asked Sarah up ahead.

Suddenly, he was free. He sank down on the ground, gasping.

'Are you all right?' Sarah shouted.

Jake staggered to his feet. His knees were trembling so hard he wasn't sure that they'd support his weight. He swallowed hard, forcing himself to take deep, calming breaths. 'Yeah, I'm fine.' It was important that he appeared calm. Any panic he showed could be contagious. He wiped away a trickle of blood from a cut on his arm. 'Let's get going.'

Olly climbed on to Jake's back and they set off along a narrow path, following Sarah. The path wound in and out between towering trees of many different varieties. At first, it led them in the direction the forest animals were taking so that they knew they were moving away from the fire. Soon though, it veered round so it was carrying them back towards the flames.

'What are we going to do?' Sarah asked.

Jake shrugged. The forest was impenetrable here. Without a machete to hack a way through to the river, they had no option but to stay on the path. But they could hear the fire approaching, though they couldn't see it yet.

'We'll have to go back,' Jake said, at last.

Sarah shook her head. 'No way. Not when we've come this far.' She marched on along the path, her back stiff with determination.

Jake went after her. 'Sarah!'

She looked round at him. 'We know there's no way through back there.'

'Maybe we missed an opening. Maybe –'

She didn't let him finish. 'I'm *not* going back.'

'But we're heading towards the fire.'

'I'm going on.' She moved forward along the path.

Jake hesitated, then went after her. 'For God's sake, Sarah –'

'The path might change direction in a minute,' she said, impatiently. 'Or the forest might thin out so we can get back on course.'

'Are we going to get burned?' Olly asked, fearfully, tightening his grip on Jake's shoulders.

'Not if I can help it,' Sarah said. She darted forward suddenly. 'Look here! There's a way through.' She pushed between two bushes. Jake put Olly down and helped him hobble after her. There was no real path but the plants mainly grew low to the ground so they could step over them. Olly hauled himself on to Jake's back again and they set off once more.

They were moving parallel to the fire now, with a line of impassable trees and bushes to the south. The crackle of burning wood filled the air and smoke hung thickly beneath the trees. It seemed to be getting hotter too. Olly's hands were sticking to Jake's bare shoulders and Jake had to keep brushing trickles of sweat from his eyes.

They peered, anxiously, between the trees as they went along. Though he couldn't see the flames yet, Jake guessed that the fire would soon reach them. 'We've got to go faster,' he said, desperately.

Jake looked north, in the direction the fire was coming from, and his blood ran cold. The fire was very close. Flames soared into the sky.

76

They leaped from tree to tree. They flickered across the ground, leaving it black and bare. Burning branches fell. Sparks spiralled into the sky, floating up with clouds of black smoke.

And the heat . . . It was almost too much to bear.

'Quicker!' Jake yelled.

They ran, hearts hammering and feet pounding. Jake clutched Olly's legs tightly so he wouldn't slide off his back. Sarah was beside him. 'Look for a way through,' Jake shouted but the deafening whoosh and crackle of the fire drowned his voice out.

Olly was shuddering. Jake guessed he was crying. He felt like crying himself. His legs could barely hold him up and Olly was a dead weight on his back. His chest was tight from the smoke, so that he could scarcely suck in a breath. His eyes were dry and sore. He blinked hard, but it didn't help. Nearer and nearer the fire came. Jake's bare skin was scorching.

On they ran, and on, frantically seeking a way through the trees to their left. Surely there had to be an opening. Forest wildlife still streamed towards the river, crossing their path, darting under the bushes in their panic. Mice, beetles, more giant centipedes. A troupe of monkeys came bounding towards them, chattering with terror. They sprang into the trees and disappeared.

Please let us find a gap, Jake prayed.

The fire drew closer still. A tree just ahead of them was burning. It was directly in their path. Jake hesitated.

'What's wrong?' Olly's voice was shrill in his ear.

Jake didn't answer. They couldn't skirt round the tree. If they did that, they'd almost be running into the heart of the fire. But if they stuck to their present course, they'd have to go right underneath it. The whole tree was ablaze. Sparks were raining down. But there was no choice. They had to go on.

'I'll go first,' Sarah shouted. She took off, dashing under the tree and out the other side.

Jake scanned the ground, making sure no roots jutted out to trip him.

Taking a deep breath, he darted forward. 'No, Jake! Stop!' Olly was screaming in his ear. He wriggled on Jake's back. Jake tried to hold him. Couldn't the stupid idiot see that they had to go quickly? All of a sudden, Olly was down. Jake whirled round, angrily. He knew Olly was scared but he'd got to trust

Jake to make the decisions. He was only doing what he thought was best.

Olly was struggling to stand up. His face was distorted with horror. He was pointing at something above Jake's head. He was yelling but Jake couldn't make out the words above the thunder and roar of the flames.

Jake looked up. A burning branch had broken loose from the tree. It was crashing down, bouncing from branch to branch, throwing up a light-show of sparks with every collision. For a moment he stared, immobilized by fear. Then his brain and body switched into gear. He hauled Olly upright and pushed him ahead, as hard as he could.

Olly stumbled a few steps and fell over. But before Jake had time to follow him, the branch landed between them exploding into shooting sparks and leaping flames. Jake hurled himself back. He hit the ground and scrambled up. Fear surged through him. He was cut off from Olly and Sarah. 'Run!' he screeched. But he didn't think his voice would carry across the noise of the fire.

The fire caught the plants that covered the ground. Flames darted towards him. The heat was unbearable. He stood his ground, his knees trembling violently. Somehow he'd got to force himself to run through those flames. He'd got to reach the others. He shut his eyes for an instant, trying to find the courage to move.

He counted in his head. One, two, three. Then he hurtled forward, eyes screwed shut, arms protecting his face and hair. Through his closed eyelids, he saw the flickering brightness. There was a moment of intense heat. A flash of pain. Then he was through.

He rolled over and over on the ground, terrified that he had been burned. He scooped up handfuls of loose soil and ash and rubbed them over himself. Above the din of the fire, he could hear Olly screaming out his name.

He opened his eyes. Sarah was bending over him, her face full of concern.

'Am I burning?'

'No, don't worry. Can you stand up?'

Shakily, Jake got to his feet. His arm hurt. His hand hurt. The hairs on his legs were singed. But he was alive. He glanced quickly at his burns. The skin on his upper arms and across his chest was very red. He knew they needed cold water but that would have to wait until they reached the river. Right now, all that mattered was that the fire was still advancing. They'd got to keep running.

Sarah hauled Olly up on to her back – Jake was in no state to help his little brother now.

CHAPTER NINE

'There!' Olly shrieked suddenly.

Sarah jerked to a stop.

'There! Look!' Olly's finger was stabbing the air, cutting through the smoke.

At first Jake couldn't see anything. His eyes were streaming and the pain in his hand was so intense he could barely think of anything else. Then he saw it. A dark gap between the trees. He dashed to it. A path led into the forest.

Weak with relief, they set off along it. There was limited space to run here – forest plants grew thickly on either side – but at least there was shelter from the sparks. And they knew they were on course for the river again because a family of mouse-like rodents was dashing along just ahead of them. Then an ant-eater lumbered by, its long thin tongue flicking in and out. They stepped off the path and let it pass, hurrying on again as soon as it had gone.

Jake badly wanted to find some water to cool his burns. They were agonizing. He examined them as he walked. The burned skin was covered in angry red blisters. Cautiously, he touched the burn on his arm. The stab of pain made him draw in his breath sharply.

'Are you OK?' Sarah asked, anxiously.

'Yeah. But I shouldn't have touched it.'

'It looks really sore,' Olly said, twisting round to see more clearly. 'And your hand. It's bright red.'

'I'm all right,' Jake said through gritted teeth.

As they moved away from the fire, the sound gradually lessened. The smoke became thinner. They began to feel more hopeful. If nothing else happened to slow them down, perhaps they could still make it.

'I hope Mum's got some food,' Olly said. 'I'm starving.'

Anxiety stabbed Jake. He'd been so

wrapped up in their escape from the flames that he'd forgotten all about their mum's plight. He hoped she and Paulo were safely out of the forest.

'Mum will be at the river, won't she, Jake?' Olly asked.

'Course she will.' She would be there. She had to be there.

The ground began to slope uphill and they trudged on in silence, needing all their breath for the climb. Their hopes rose with each step though. Surely they were on the home stretch now. They'd probably be able to see the river when they reached the top of this rise.

Higher and higher they climbed. Jake went on ahead. Sarah laboured after him with Olly on her back. He felt guilty but there was nothing he could do to help her – carrying his brother on his back would rip his dry and brittle skin apart for sure.

The ground was rocky now with only a thin layer of soil. Trees were stunted and their knobbly roots stretched out along the ground. At last, they left the trees behind. A few misshapen bushes still clung to the steep slope but even they dwindled as they climbed higher. Eventually they reached a place where nothing grew at all.

The air was clear here. Jake stopped for a moment. He took a deep breath, trying to get the taste of the smoke out of his mouth and some fresh air into his lungs.

Sarah and Olly caught Jake up, then went on ahead to the crest of the hill. Sarah lowered Olly on to a wide, flat rock.

'Come and look!' Olly called.

Jake clambered up to them. They were on a narrow ridge above the forest. The trees were hidden by a blanket of smoke that hung in the air below them like a red-black fog. Tongues of brilliant flame licked through it, shooting high into the sky. Beyond the fire, where the smoke was thinner, everything was blackened and burned. Further off still, the lush green of the forest appeared untouched.

'We'll be OK here,' Jake said. 'Rock doesn't burn.'

'We're not staying here, are we?' Olly asked, plaintively.

Jake shrugged. 'Probably.'

Olly caught Jake's hand and pulled himself up. He looked ahead, down the other side of the hill. 'There's the river!'

Jake and Sarah turned to see. Olly was right – the river was a broad, silver ribbon below. To reach it, they'd have to climb down a steep slope and get through another band of trees.

'Let's go down there and find Mum,' said Olly, excitedly.

It didn't look far but, all the same, Jake didn't want to risk it. 'Better to stay here until the fire's out, Olly,' he said. Jake sighed. 'It's too dangerous to go on. You know how quickly the fire spreads.'

Olly's eyes filled with tears. 'But I want Mum,' he said.

'I know, but we'll be safe here.'

The tears trickled down Olly's cheeks.

'We'll go down to the river when the fire's gone out.'

'The fire could go on for days!' Olly said angrily.

Jake glanced at Sarah.

'I don't know what's best,' she said. 'The plan has always been to reach the river. Although we're safer up here. But Olly's right, it could go on for days. And we've got nothing to eat or drink.'

'See.' Olly wiped away his tears with the back of his hand. 'We'll have to go down to the river.'

Jake frowned. 'I'm not sure. The fire's come close to catching us already. I think we should stay up here.'

'No!' Olly's tears spilled over again. 'I don't want to stay here.'

'It'll be all right, Jake,' Sarah said. 'You can see how close we are to the river. And you need to get those burns looked at. And there's Olly's ankle, too. He's in agony.'

'But suppose the rain forest's difficult to get through? Suppose we hit a dead-end again?' Jake didn't want to think about what might happen. 'We'd nearly had it back there.'

'We can make it!' Olly said. 'Tell him, Sarah.'

Sarah looked back at the fire. 'I reckon we'll outrun it.' She smiled encouragingly at Jake. 'It'll be OK, you'll see.'

Jake didn't return her smile. Part of him wanted to go on to the river. He desperately wanted to know if his mum was all right. And being stuck on the top of a rocky hill, for days on end, waiting for the fire to die down sounded pretty grim. But the idea of having to outrun the fire again frightened him. They'd seen its awesome power already. So far they'd been lucky – they'd only got an injured ankle and a few burns to show for their close encounter with the flames. But how long would their luck hold?

'Me and Sarah want to go on,' Olly said, 'so you're outnumbered.'

'It's not as simple as that, Olly –'

'Don't worry, Jake,' Sarah cut in. 'It'll be fine, you'll see.' She nudged Olly. 'I can't carry you down this slope – it's too steep. We'll have to slide down on our bums. I'll race you to the trees.'

She and Olly started to slide on the loose stones and soil.

'Wait!' Jake called. 'Wait! We should stay here.'

They were gathering speed.

Jake sighed. Olly was right: he was outnumbered. And he couldn't let Olly go off without him. Jake slid after them.

He caught them up on the edge of the forest. Sarah got to her feet, grinning. She helped Olly clamber on to her back.

'Do you want me to carry him for a while?' Jake asked. His burns still hurt but it didn't seem fair to make Sarah do all the work. Especially when Olly wasn't even her brother. He felt he had to make the effort.

'No. I'm getting used to lugging him around,' Sarah said.

The slope was much gentler here and they soon found a path that led in the direction of the river. 'I can't wait to see Mum,' Olly said, as they jogged along. He sounded more like his usual, chirpy self.

'Me too,' Jake said. *Just as long as she's there*, he added silently.

At last the ground levelled out and the nature of the forest began to change again. The ground became damp and walking on it was like treading on a giant sponge. Their feet sank in a little and fallen leaves glued themselves around their boots in sodden, heavy masses.

The trees were different here too. They weren't as tall as others they'd seen and they had wide, buttressed roots. Though the trees were quite widely spaced, their branches were long and they touched those of the trees growing alongside them. 'It's the vérzea,' Sarah said. 'It floods in the wet season but at this time of year the water slowly evaporates.'

The further they went, the wetter the ground became. Soon they were splashing through muddy puddles. 'We must be nearly at the river,' Olly cried, eagerly.

They reached a stream. The dark water wound in and out between the trees. It was too wide to jump but it wasn't deep, so Jake and Sarah waded in. The water was warm.

Jake stopped for a moment in midstream to dip his burned hand in. He splashed some water on his blistered arm, too.

'Does it hurt a lot?' Sarah asked.

He shrugged. 'It's not too bad.'

Sarah and Olly crossed the stream. 'Come on, Jake,' Olly called. 'I want something to eat.'

Jake waded after them, his feet sinking into the soft mud of the stream-bed. He clambered out on to the bank and they went on, their wet boots squelching as they walked. The ground became boggier. It was an effort to pull their feet out of the mud and their progress became worryingly slow.

Jake scanned the ground, searching, in vain, for a solid path. The bog seemed to go on forever, broken only by trees. And the noise of the fire was growing again. Jake looked back. The flames were gaining on them. Through the trees he could just make out the flicker of orange flames. Panic boiled up inside him. This time the fire would overtake them. The mud was slowing them down, trapping them. His heart beat frenziedly. His hands grew clammy with fear. They had to go faster. But how could they hurry across this squelching mud?

Jake wrenched an ankle free with his good hand. He took another step. As he hauled on his other ankle, he looked back again at the fire. It was closer than ever now. He battled to stay calm. They'd never escape if he gave way to the fear that threatened to overwhelm him. But what could they do?

'The fire won't burn where the ground's wet, will it, Jake?' Olly asked, apprehensively.

'I shouldn't think so.' Jake took a deep breath, trying to keep his voice steady. It would probably spread through the trees though, he thought, despairingly, even if it couldn't run along the ground. He shuddered, imagining how it would feel to be directly below it as it roared overhead, showering them with sparks and bits of burning tree.

Jake moved ahead of Sarah, still searching for an easier route, wishing they'd stayed on the hilltop. Every step they took was laboured, their ankles gripped by oozing mud. He could feel it inside his boots, squishing between his toes.

'Jake!' Sarah's voice was shrill with fear. Jake turned sharply. She was almost knee deep in mud. As he watched, she sank a little further.

'Get off, Olly!' Jake yelled. His brother's

weight must be pushing her deeper than him. She'd never get out with Olly on her back.

Olly slid down. He splashed on to the mud. 'Move as quickly as you can,' Jake cried, 'so you don't start sinking, too.'

'What about my ankle?'

'You'll have to manage.' Jake knew it sounded heartless but what else could he say? He wrenched one foot free of the clinging mud and moved towards Olly.

'Keep away!' Sarah shouted. 'You'll get stuck too, if you come any closer!'

Olly limped across the mud towards Jake, gritting his teeth against the pain in his ankle. Being so much smaller and lighter prevented him from sinking as quickly.

Sarah was battling vainly to get clear of the mud. She clasped one knee with both hands and pulled hard but her leg wouldn't come free. If anything, her efforts made her sink deeper.

'Come on!' Jake tried to encourage her.

'I can't get out.' She glanced back fearfully at the trees. Jake followed her gaze.

The fire was getting closer.

Jake saw whole trees ablaze now. Sparks were dropping on to the mud less than 100 metres away. Spindly flames leaped from branch to branch. He could feel the heat growing too. Even at this distance it made his skin prickle.

Sarah wrenched at her legs again. 'Help me, Jake! Help me!'

'It's all right,' Jake called. 'I'll get you out.' But he could see that she was sinking lower. The mud was past her knees now.

Jake looked round, frantically. There had to be something he could use to get her out. A fallen branch was lying on the ground. He snatched it up and reached out towards Sarah with it. It was way too short. Pulling one foot out of the bog, he took a tentative step towards her. If he could get a bit closer, perhaps he could reach her. He took another step. And another. But the mud became softer as he moved towards her. He could feel it sucking at his feet, dragging him down.

He threw down the branch and retreated. Going on would be pointless. If he got stuck as well, they'd never escape and the fire would get them all. He had to think about Olly too.

The mud was halfway up Sarah's thighs now. Jake fought down the panic that boiled inside him. He'd got to think clearly, to work out what to do. He couldn't get any closer to her – that was obvious. And he couldn't find a branch long enough to reach her. He scanned the surrounding area frantically. Surely there had to be something he could use to pull her out.

'We ought to go to the river and get some people to help us,' Olly suggested.

Jake shook his head. 'It'll take too long.' He wished he could find a safe place for Olly to wait but there was nothing but mud all around them.

'Help, Jake!' Sarah screamed. 'Get me out! I've got to get out!' She lunged forward, her hands beating the mud, her face distorted with terror.

'Sarah!' Jake had never seen her like this. She'd always been so cool and sensible before. 'Calm down!' He had to shout to make her listen. 'I'm going to get you out.'

Tears were coursing down her face.

And she was still sinking.

The mud had reached her waist now.

A wave of new horror swept over Jake. The fire wasn't their only enemy. This wasn't ordinary mud. This was a real bog, a deadly quagmire that sucked people down and suffocated them.

And Sarah was at its mercy.

CHAPTER TEN

Fear tore through Jake. 'Keep your arms clear of the mud,' he called, as he watched Sarah struggling to raise herself up. 'And don't move.' He'd seen on a film once that keeping still stopped you from sinking fast if you fell into a bog.

Olly watched from marginally more solid ground a few metres away. 'Think of something, Jake! Help her!'

'I'm trying,' cried Jake. But how was he going to reach her? He looked round despairingly. Creepers hung from the trees, looping down to touch the bog in places. They looked like ropes. Perhaps Jake could use one to pull Sarah out? He headed for a tree, moving frustratingly slowly, having to drag his feet out of the clinging mud with every step.

'Don't leave me,' Sarah sobbed.

'I'm not.' He looked back over his shoulder. She was still sinking and the fire was closer than ever. There wasn't much time left.

He turned away again. He couldn't bear to see the terror in Sarah's face. 'I'm going to get you out,' he promised. He was almost at the tree now. Two more steps and the creeper was in his hands. He hauled on it, heedless of the pain in his burned hand. It didn't budge. He yanked again, harder than ever. The creeper broke free. A tangle of flat, rope-like strands cascaded down from the tree. They were linked together by a knot of roots.

Jake snatched it up. He tried to wrench off one of the stems of creeper but it was too strong and he couldn't separate it. He gave up and gathered up the whole thing. Then he battled through the mud again. Sarah was chest deep in the mire now. Her face was deathly white.

'Hold on,' Jake panted. 'I'm coming.'

'I'm scared, Jake.' She wasn't panicking any more, Jake could see. But there was a look of terrible resignation on her face, as though she knew she was going to die.

'Don't give up,' he begged.

The fire was getting closer. Jake could see the orange glow reflected in Sarah's eyes. Burning trees cracked and the whoosh of the advancing flames grew louder by the second.

Jake moved as close to her as he dared. He coiled up the creeper, then, keeping a tight hold on one end, he hurled the other out over the bog towards her. It uncoiled as it went, spreading out its stems in all directions. He willed it to reach her. It fell short and lay across the mud like a long-limbed, skinny octopus with the root-ball for a body.

Jake pulled the creeper in. 'I'll get it to you this time.' He was shaking uncontrollably. He took a deep breath and threw the creeper again. The end of one stem landed close to Sarah. 'Grab it!' he yelled. She stretched out one arm. The creeper was close but she couldn't quite touch it. The movement made her sink deeper into the bog.

Jake's hands felt big and clumsy as he coiled the creeper in again. He was fighting to control his rising panic. He'd got to get his aim right. There wasn't time for another failure. The mud was up to Sarah's shoulders.

And the fire . . . he couldn't bring himself to look at it. There was no time for that. But the light from the flames was throwing ever-changing patterns across the swamp. The smoke that drifted round him was tinged with orange. And the noise was deafening.

Sweat dripped down Jake's forehead and into his eyes. He wiped it away impatiently, looking across the bog at Sarah, measuring the distance. He threw the coil of creeper again. It snaked out across the bog. One stem landed in front of her. She seized it. 'I've got it!'

'Hold on tight. I'm going to pull you out.'

He wrapped the creeper round his hands and pulled. It cut into his burned skin. The pain made him gasp. But he kept on pulling. He wasn't going to give up, no matter how much it hurt.

But Sarah wasn't moving. He couldn't budge her. The pull of the thick mud was too great. He looped the creeper round his waist and pulled again, leaning back like the anchorman in a tug of war.

Suddenly Jake felt Olly's arms round him. They pulled together.

Slowly, slowly, Sarah began to move. She rose out of the bog like a horror-film monster. The mud tried to hold her, but against the pull of the rope it slowly slithered down her body and gave her up with a pop. Sarah was now lying on top of the mud, clutching the creeper with both hands. Jake and Olly pulled again. She edged towards them, snaking across the oozing mud. Her increased surface area stopped her from sinking again.

Something plopped down beside Jake. He heard it sizzle and he knew it was a spark. He pulled harder than ever: there was so little time. More sparks fell. One hit his exposed shoulder. He barely noticed the pain. His mind was too focused on pulling.

'Jake!' Olly's scream of terror cut through the fire's roaring. Jake looked past Sarah. The trees directly behind her were alight.

Fear twisted like a knife in Jake's chest. His heart pounded so hard, he thought it would come bursting out. He hauled Sarah in. She staggered to her feet. She was caked in mud and she stank worse than some of the chemical concoctions Jake had created in the science lab at school. 'Let's get out of here,' she gasped.

But it was already too late. Flames raced along the branches above them, cracking and hissing. Bark burst open. The air was full of sparks and blinding, choking smoke.

Jake's mind was numb with terror. *How could they escape this inferno?*

Jake struggled to control his fear. He'd got to concentrate on finding a way out. He clasped his trembling hands tightly together, searching his mind for an idea that would save them.

And suddenly he knew the answer. 'Mud!' he cried. 'Cover yourselves with mud.'

He scooped up a handful of mud and dumped it on top of his head. He patted it thickly over his face and hair. Scooping up more, he heaped it on his shoulders. He let it run down his back. He covered his neck, chest and legs. The mud wouldn't burn so maybe it would protect them from the fire. He knew it wasn't much of a defence but it was better than nothing.

Sarah had been staring at Jake in bewilderment but now her eyes registered comprehension. 'Yes! Yes! Do it, Olly!' She covered her head and arms in mud, leaving a ring of white skin around her eyes. The rest of her was already muddy from her dip in the bog.

Jake helped Olly smother himself with mud, then he slung him over his shoulder in a fireman's lift. The layer of mud helped lessen

Jake's pain as he held Olly against his burned skin. Olly struggled to get down but Jake held him tight. He was safest with his head down, away from the blazing branches.

Jake looked round, quickly identifying the safest route between the burning tree trunks. 'This way!' He pointed with his free hand.

He and Sarah moved forward, hauling their feet out of the oozing mud, taking enormous strides so they could cover the ground more quickly. Burning leaves and twigs showered down from the blazing branches overhead. On every side smoke frothed out of burning tree trunks and boiled upwards, seeking a way through the flaming branches.

Soon the ground became firmer. Jake's hopes lifted a little – at least they could run now.

Despite their exhaustion they darted forward, dodging round blazing trees, ducking under branches engulfed in flames. On and on, through the smoke and heat, fighting to get ahead of the fire.

Olly's head bumped against Jake's back. Sarah was beside Jake. Running, running. They were determined to win. They were moving faster than the fire now, through sparks that swarmed around them like fireflies.

They reached the dense forest just ahead of the fire. They found a path almost immediately and darted along it.

On and on they ran. Jake was almost doubled over. Not just with Olly's weight over his shoulder but with a terrible, crippling stitch in his side. But he wouldn't give in to it. He had to go on. And on.

They sped along in silence, their heads ringing with the sounds of destruction behind them. They ran like robots, their minds blank, every fibre of their bodies intent on survival.

And suddenly, without warning – the river was right in front of them.

They lurched to a halt and stared at the vast expanse of grey water, hardly able to believe that they'd reached it at last. Monkeys, mice, brightly coloured frogs, tree porcupines and countless other creatures that Jake didn't recognize were all streaming out of the forest, hurling themselves into the water and swimming away from the bank.

Jake waited for euphoria to flood over him. They'd done it! They'd reached the river!

He looked along it.

There was nothing but forest for as far as he could see in both directions.

There was nobody in sight.

'We've got to find the jetty,' Sarah cried. 'The rescue boats will be there.' They turned left and stumbled along beside the river, clambering over leaning trees whose branches reached out over the water. Rounding a bend in the river, they stopped in dismay.

There was the jetty and the cluster of wooden huts on the bank that they'd seen the previous day. It was where they had arrived.

But it was deserted.

Jake scanned the river disbelievingly. Where were the boats? There *had* to be boats. They'd come so far, fought so hard to survive. And now ... Tears of rage and frustration pricked the backs of his eyes. All their efforts had been pointless. They were trapped between the fire and the river.

Olly thumped Jake's back. 'Where is everybody?'

Jake set him down. 'I don't know,' he said quietly.

Olly turned on him. 'Where's Mum?'

Jake shook his head. 'She's not here, Olly.'

'Where are the boats?' Olly demanded.

'There aren't any.'

Olly's shoulders slumped. 'You said ... You said there'd be a boat. You promised.' He started to cry.

'It's not my fault,' Jake snapped. 'I thought –' He broke off. What was the point of arguing?

Olly sobbed more loudly and ran into Sarah's arms. She hugged him tightly, trying to comfort him.

'Olly . . .' Jake began. But what could he say? They'd come all this way – for nothing.

CHAPTER ELEVEN

Jake stiffened and determined not to give up so soon. They weren't dead yet. 'Let's go to the jetty,' he said, firmly. 'Come on. Perhaps a boat will come along. They'll see us better there.' He sounded calm but, inside, he was in despair. Everyone probably thought they were dead. No wonder the boats had gone without them.

He picked Olly up and trudged along the bank with him. The ground was alive with insects. Shiny, green beetles were streaming out of the forest. Black ants, as big as earwigs, darted among them. They scuttled to the water's edge, then drew back, searching for some other safety route.

The flames came ever closer, ceaselessly devouring the forest in its path. Sparks fell all around them from the canopy high in the sky. Soon the fire would reach the river along the ground and they would have nowhere left to run to.

'We'll have to get in the water,' Sarah said. 'The fire won't touch us there.'

Jake scanned the river. He knew there was danger in the water. There'd be snakes out there, swimming for their lives, and piranha fish that could strip your bones in seconds. And caymans.

'Come on, Jake.' Sarah tugged at his arm. 'We've got to get in the water. It's our only chance.'

A troupe of squirrel monkeys came screaming out of the forest. They swung out over the river, hanging from jutting branches by their tails, then splashed into the water. As they floundered away from the bank, Jake saw the huge, knobbly, black shape of a cayman gliding towards them.

'No. Wait!' shouted Jake. 'Look!'

Using its long body and powerful tail, the cayman separated one monkey from the rest. It opened its mouth, revealing sharp, white teeth. The monkey shrieked. It lunged backwards, pawing at the water with its tiny hands, trying desperately to escape. The cayman struck. It scooped up the monkey and its enormous mouth snapped shut. The cayman sank below the surface, taking its victim with it.

A wave of nausea swept over Jake. They could stay on land and be burned to death or they could get into the river and be ripped apart by caymans. That was the only choice left to them. To burn or to be eaten.

Olly clung to Jake, sobbing, his face buried in Jake's shoulder. Sarah's fingers bit into Jake's arm. 'What are we going to do?'

'Get to the jetty. It'll give us a bit longer.' They couldn't just give up. They had to keep on fighting. Right to the end.

They ran again, shielding their eyes from the flurries of stinging sparks. Small fires were breaking out ahead of them but they plunged on, skirting the flames and ignoring the uncomfortable heat.

Jake's gaze was fixed on the jetty. Through the haze of orange-tinged smoke, he saw a movement. He blinked, trying to see more clearly. Someone was running to the end of the jetty. Jake's heart leaped into his mouth. Perhaps it was Mum. Perhaps she'd stayed behind when the boats had left. Perhaps she'd insisted on waiting for them. Jake felt a sob rise up inside him. He wanted her to be safe, not here facing such extreme danger.

A second figure emerged from one of the huts. He followed the first. Jake was sure it was a man from the way he ran.

Jake, Sarah and Olly reached the huts. One of them was on fire. Flames streaked through the roof and through the window. They rippled up the plank walls, sending a stream of black smoke pouring into the sky. Jake dived past it and darted out on to the jetty. Sarah was right behind him.

The jetty was only ten or so metres long. The figures were at the far end, watching them. Jake could see, now, that both of them were men. They were dressed identically in blue overalls and clumpy, brown boots.

Halfway along the jetty, Sarah caught his arm and jerked him to a stop. 'Look at their overalls. They're loggers. From the Logan Corporation.'

'So?'

'So they're the ones we came here to stop.'

Jake frowned. 'They might be able to help us. Maybe they've got a radio. Maybe they know when a boat's going to come.'

Sarah shook her head. 'I'm not going anywhere near *them*.'

'Don't be an idiot.'

Her eyes flashed angrily. 'People like that are wrecking the world.'

'So you won't accept help from them? Even if it means we'll all be saved?'

Sarah hesitated. 'Think of what they've done to the rain forest, Jake. Think of all the trees they've destroyed.'

Jake could hardly believe what he was hearing. 'The forest is on fire,' he screamed. 'We're in terrible danger. Do you want to die?'

'How do you know they can help us?' Sarah threw back.

'I don't know. But it's worth finding out.'

She sighed. 'It feels wrong to even speak to them.' She looked back at the fire and shook her head. 'I suppose we don't have any choice.'

'Too right we don't.' Jake moved towards the two men and set Olly down. 'Hallo. Can you help us? Do you know if a boat's coming?'

'Where've you kids come from?' one of them asked. He was a tall, solidly built man with grey, thinning hair. He sounded American.

Jake pointed back towards the fire. 'We came through there. We got lost in the forest.' He didn't mention the fact that they'd been planning to invade the lumber camp. There was no point stirring up trouble.

The man shook his head sadly. 'You've missed the boats. We all have.' He looked out across the river and shrugged. 'And it's one hell of a way to the evacuation centre.'

'How are we going to get away?' Olly sobbed.

The second man patted his shoulder. He was younger than his companion, small and wiry with black hair. '*Vai ficar tudo bem*,' he said.

Jake guessed he was speaking Portuguese but he had no idea what it meant. 'What's he saying?' he asked.

'He said, we're gonna be OK,' the American told him. They all knew he was only saying it to try and reassure Olly. 'I'm Tex and this is Luis,' the American went on. 'You?'

Jake told him.

A spark landed on the jetty. Olly jerked away from it, quivering with fear. Luis stamped it out.

Jake knelt down and held his brother against his body. He could feel him trembling.

'Why didn't you go in one of the boats?' Jake asked, at last.

'Too full,' Tex said. 'Someone had to stay behind. They said they'd send someone back, but I'm not sure when it'll be. The fire has spread faster than anyone could have imagined.'

'You don't mean . . .?' Sarah began.

Jake looked at the two men in astonishment. Had they really volunteered to stay behind, even though they suspected the boats wouldn't get back for them in time?

Tex shrugged. 'Them boats were too low in the water as it was. Even an extra –' He broke off as a storm of sparks showered them. Two landed in Olly's hair. Jake flicked them away before they could set it alight.

Tex and Luis ran around stamping on the sparks. Jake and Sarah joined in. Olly stayed where he was, balancing on his good leg and watching, wide-eyed with fear. A flame sprang up at the far end of the jetty, where it joined the land.

Jake darted to it. He stamped it out but more fires were bursting into life around him. He carried on stamping, knowing, in his heart, that he was fighting a losing battle. The flames would destroy the jetty in the end and they'd be forced into the water. He looked at the river bank, wondering whether they'd be safer there, but all the huts were ablaze now.

As he watched, one of the huts gave way. The roof caved in. The walls teetered, then fell. One of them crashed towards Jake. He sprang back as it thundered close by the jetty, smashing into flaming fragments.

Tex and Luis came running to help him but the fire was too widespread to be stamped out this time.

Jake knelt down and scooped river water up in his hands. He tossed it on to a piece of burning plank. A few of the flames fizzed and went out but he could see it was hopeless. It would take an army of firefighters to extinguish so many flames.

Tex caught his blistered arm and dragged Jake to his feet. 'Come on, kid.' Gasping with pain, Jake pulled free.

'*Voce queimou o seu braco*,' Luis said.

'You've burned your arm?' Tex said. 'Sorry.' He ushered Jake to the end of the jetty, where Sarah was still stamping out falling sparks. Olly was kneeling on the wooden planking, shielding his head with his arms. Jake knelt beside him and put his arm round Olly's shaking shoulders. He wanted to comfort him. But what words could he say? He could hardly promise that things would turn out all right now.

Jake gazed out across the grey water. He willed a boat to come. Surely it was their only hope of survival now.

The jetty was burning strongly. Flames devoured the planks, throwing up a thick pall of smoke. Slowly, the fire advanced. It was only a few metres away now. Sparks streaked at them, stinging unprotected skin and threatening to set fire to clothes and hair. And the heat was intense.

Jake knew the time had nearly come when they'd have to choose between the fire and the caymans. But how could you make a choice like that?

'What are we –?' he began.

Luis held up a hand to silence him.

They listened. There was a whirring noise above their heads. They looked up. A helicopter appeared through the smoke.

'Help!' they bellowed. '*Socorro!*'

The helicopter screeched past.

'No!' Sarah screamed. 'No! Don't leave us!'

Olly's face collapsed as he watched the helicopter move away.

Everyone fell silent. Jake stared after it,

disbelievingly. To feel his emotions swing from wild hope to total despair was torture. He watched the helicopter veer out over the river. It turned slowly. Then it headed straight for them.

They yelled again. Had the crew seen them? Jake waited, weak with dread. The helicopter hovered directly overhead. Its rotor blades sent the smoke puffing away across the sky in dark, woolly edged clouds. The flames, temporarily cowed by the down draught, flattened themselves against the jetty.

A door opened in the helicopter. A man looked out. He waved a gloved hand at them. He seemed to be shouting something but they couldn't hear above the clatter of the rotor blades. A moment later, a harness came down, attached to a rope. A feeling of elation rushed through Jake.

Tex grabbed it. He wrapped it round Olly and fastened it.

Olly clung to Jake. Jake prised his hands away. His brother swung out over the water, rising steadily towards the helicopter. His eyes were tight shut. He looked petrified.

Jake turned to Sarah. 'You're next,' he bellowed, trying to make his voice heard above the helicopter's din.

She shook her head and pointed to Jake's burns.

'I'm not arguing about it, Sarah. You're going next and that's that.' He didn't know whether she could hear him or not but he wasn't going to give way.

The winchman hauled Olly into the helicopter. A moment later, the harness dropped again. Tex caught it and held it out to Sarah.

Sarah looked questioningly at Jake. He shook his head and moved away. When he looked back, she was buckling the harness tightly. She raised a hand to the winchman. A moment later she was lifted off her feet.

The flames were so near now that there was hardly any space on the jetty and the heat was unbearable. 'Can't stay here no more,' Tex yelled.

He knelt down and prised up a loose plank from the jetty. Wrenching it free, he thrust it into Jake's hands. 'It's for them alligators.'

Jake winced. His burned hand was so painful, he almost let the plank fall, but somehow he managed to hold on to it. Luis had worked a plank loose too. He stood on the very end of the jetty, gripping it tightly, staring into the water. Tex wrenched another plank free.

Jake looked up at the helicopter. The winchman was leaning out, ready to pull Sarah in. But he knew the harness wouldn't reach them again until the jetty was engulfed by fire. He swallowed hard. They'd got to get into deep water where the flames couldn't touch them. But the image of the poor squirrel monkey was imprinted on his mind. He couldn't forget it. That terrifying, black monster . . . Those razor-sharp teeth . . . In spite of the pain in his hand, he tightened his grip on the plank. It was his only protection.

'Let's go!' Tex cried. He leaped into the river. Luis followed. Jake shut his eyes, trying to psych himself up. The heat was intolerable. He could feel it scorching his back, singeing his hair. He leaped forward.

The water was only waist-deep but Jake sank, up to his ankles, in soft mud. As he waded away from the jetty, something brushed his bare knee. He sprang back, suddenly frightened. Peering into the water, he saw fronds of dark weed. He laughed hysterically. It was only a plant!

Jake moved on, keeping a wary eye out for caymans and snakes. Tex and Luis positioned themselves on either side of him. He was grateful for that.

'Here it comes,' Tex shouted. The harness was descending again. Jake watched it longingly. He was desperate to reach the safety of the helicopter but Tex and Luis deserved to be rescued too.

Tex caught the harness and held it out to Jake.

Jake shook his head. 'You or Luis can go next.'

'You get yourself in there, boy.'

Jake didn't argue. He slipped the harness on gratefully, buckled it up and waved to the winchman. *Let them be all right*, he prayed, as he was lifted out of the water.

He watched the two men as he rose. They were standing back to back, surveying the river, their planks at the ready. Then he saw it. A black shape, cutting through the water towards them. It didn't look as big as the cayman that had killed the monkey but he couldn't be sure from this height.

'Look out!' he yelled. 'Luis! Look out! It's heading right for you.'

Luis turned to face the cayman. He raised the plank. Tex moved beside him, ready for the monster too. It came nearer, powering through the water, flicking its tail. It was almost on them when the two men brought the planks crashing down. Water splashed up in a froth of white. The cayman dived beneath the surface.

Tex's voice drifted up to Jake: 'Where'd he go?' He was peering into the water.

For a moment, Jake couldn't see the cayman. He watched fearfully, terrified that Luis or Tex would suddenly be dragged down or that the gaping jaws would surface behind them. Then he spotted it. It was speeding away from them. Relief swept over him. 'It's going!' he yelled.

He looked up. He'd almost reached the helicopter now. The clattering of its rotor blades was deafening. The winchman was reaching out to him. He caught Jake's good arm and hauled him inside. Jake took off the harness, his fingers fumbling with the buckles in his haste. The winchman lowered it again.

The helicopter was gloomy inside. The cockpit was separated from them by a screen and there were only four small windows in this back section. Sarah was looking out of one of them. Olly was sitting on the far side, leaning against the wall. A young, blonde woman was kneeling beside him, examining his ankle. 'Is he all right?' Jake asked. He moved across to them, feeling the engine's vibration through his feet.

She looked up at Jake, smiling and nodding. 'OK. Not much problem.' She spoke with a Brazilian accent.

Jake joined Sarah at the window. He pressed his forehead against the glass. The fire still raged along the riverbank and the jetty. Luis was buckling himself into the harness. Tex was scanning the river, rotating slowly, watching for caymans. The winchman turned a handle fixed to the side of the helicopter. Luis began to rise out of the water.

Moments later, the winchman dragged him inside. Hurriedly, he unfastened the harness and within seconds it was on its way back to Tex. 'I thought you'd had it when I saw that cayman,' Jake said, as Luis scrambled to his feet.

He smiled and shrugged, showing he hadn't understood.

Jake turned back to the window. Tex was pulling on the harness. He raised a hand and the winchman began to wind him in. The helicopter was already moving away. In less than a minute Tex was hauled safely inside.

The vibration of the helicopter increased. It lurched upwards and then swung round, powering away from the fire.

CHAPTER TWELVE

The evacuation centre was packed. Jake looked out at it as the helicopter came in to land. It was made up of a scattering of flat-roofed brick buildings that stood alongside the river. A wooden jetty stretched out into the water. At the end of it a large boat was taking in people. Two more boats were waiting for a space at the jetty. A queue of people, some clutching small children or suitcases, snaked along the jetty and round the side of one of the buildings.

More people scurried back and forth between the buildings or ran along beside the queue waiting for the boats, scanning the crowd. Jake guessed they were searching for missing family members. Others stood about aimlessly or sat on the ground – probably relieved to still be alive.

A crowd of people wearing protective overalls and helmets with visors was grouped around a row of helicopters. They stood on a large area of grass behind the buildings.

'Firefighters,' Tex said.

'Can you see Mum, Jake?' Olly asked, getting awkwardly to his feet.

Jake peered out again. 'Not yet. But there's loads of people down there.' His spirits rose a little. If so many people had been rescued, surely Mum would be among them. Jake was exhausted – they all were. He struggled to stay alert despite feeling relieved that he no longer had the responsibility of leading them out of danger.

The helicopter touched down with a bump beside the others. The engine stopped and the winchman opened the door. Jake and Sarah helped Olly to the door. They thanked the winchman and the medic and said goodbye to Luis and Tex.

Jake and Sarah jumped down. They lifted Olly out of the helicopter. 'Do you want another piggyback?' Jake asked.

Olly seized Jake's arm and hobbled a few

steps. 'My ankle doesn't feel so bad now that it's strapped up. I'll be OK as long as I can lean on you.'

They headed for the jetty, frantically checking out the milling people. They came across a tap attached to the outside of a café and washed off the worst of the mud from their bodies. Jake could see families sitting at tables, eating and drinking.

Emergency food and drink had been laid on for evacuees from the forest and they grabbed some fruit and water.

'What is this place?' Sarah asked. 'Why's there a café in the middle of nowhere?'

Olly pointed to a sign positioned near the jetty. It was written in several languages. The English version said, The Gateway to the Rain Forest.

'Tourists must stop here,' Jake said. 'I bet it's not usually an evacuation centre.'

Next to the café was a smaller building with pictures of rain forest animals and birds painted on the brickwork. A multi-lingual sign outside told them that walking tours of the rain forest left once an hour. As they drew nearer, pushing their way through the crowd, they saw that a sheet bearing a red cross had been draped above the door.

'The emergency medical centre,' Sarah said. 'Do you want to get your burns looked at?'

Jake shook his head. 'I'll do it later. But we ought to go in there and look for Mum.'

'Sarah!' The voice came from somewhere in the crowd.

'That's my dad!' Sarah cried.

A tall, bearded man emerged from the throng. He ran to her and swept her off her feet. 'Thank God you're safe!'

Sarah's arms went round his neck. 'Where's Mum? And Hannah?'

'Down on the jetty, looking for you.' He held her close. 'We thought you'd been left behind. We couldn't all get on the same boat. Hannah and your mum went on the first one and I thought you were with them. Your mother thought you were with me on the second boat. How did you get here?'

'In a helicopter. I'll tell you about it later.'

'But you're all right?' Her father set her down and studied her anxiously. He pushed her matted hair away from her eyes.

'I'm fine, Dad.'

He smiled, then glanced at Jake and

Olly. His face turned serious. 'You're Gill Weston's boys, aren't you? The ones who disappeared?'

Jake nodded. 'Do you know where she is? Have you seen her?'

He shook his head, his face stricken. 'She realized you were missing just before midnight. We split up into search parties and searched the area around the camp for hours. Then around half-past four we spotted the fire.' He shivered. 'We got back to camp and everyone cleared out.'

'And Mum?' Jake asked.

'She wouldn't leave without you, so Paulo agreed to stay with her.' He laid a comforting hand on Jake's shoulder. 'I don't think they made it to the jetty in time for the rescue boats.'

His words were shocking, crushing. Jake could hardly take it in. His mum could still be out in the burning rain forest somewhere. Olly began to cry. Tears welled up in Jake's eyes too.

'She might have got out a different way,' Sarah said. 'Maybe a helicopter's bringing her in.'

'They're searching along the river now,' added Sarah's dad.

'Or maybe she was in one of the boats and my dad didn't see her.'

Jake clutched at Sarah's suggestion. He couldn't bear the idea that he'd never see his mother again.

'That burn looks nasty,' Sarah's dad said, inspecting Jake's hand. 'You ought to get it looked at.'

'I'll do it later.' Jake blinked his tears away. 'After we've found Mum.'

He heard the whirr of a helicopter and looked up hopefully, praying that it would be carrying his mum and Paulo. The helicopter was taking off though. It was the first in the fleet of firefighters. As it rose into the sky, another took off behind it. And another. And another. The crowd cheered.

'We'll help you look for your mum,' Sarah's dad shouted above the noise of the helicopters. 'Sarah and I will try the jetty and the buildings over on the right. You try inside the medical centre and then go off to the left. We'll meet back here.'

Jake nodded, glad to let somebody else take control. His mind felt numb. All he could think about was his mum. Where was she? What had happened to her? He prayed that she was all right.

'Let's have a look at this crowd, Olly,' he said. 'For all we know, Mum might be in the middle of it, waiting to get into the medical centre.'

Jake stood up and helped Olly climb on to a low wall, taking care not to jar his ankle, then jumped up beside him. He looked the people over, scrutinizing every face. He recognized several of the protesters from the camp but their mum wasn't there.

A wave of bitter disappointment swept over Jake. He wanted to find her so badly. He jumped down from the wall and lifted Olly down. 'She wasn't there, was she?' Olly said, tearfully.

'She might be inside,' Jake said with more confidence than he felt. 'Maybe she's looking for us.' He forced a smile, trying to reassure Olly. 'Come on. We've got to keep looking.'

They pushed through the crowd but so many people had congregated round the door that they couldn't reach it.

'Down here,' Jake said, steering Olly into a narrow passageway between the medical centre and the next building. There was a door halfway along. Jake opened it and ushered Olly inside.

The building was packed. People stood in groups, chatting, waiting to see a doctor. Most of them didn't look too badly hurt and Jake guessed that the urgent cases were treated elsewhere.

A tired-looking woman was sitting at a desk near the door. Jake and Olly squeezed through the throng to her.

'Do you speak English?' Jake asked.

She smiled. 'A little.' She spoke with a strong Brazilian accent.

'We're looking for our mother. She's called Gill Weston.'

The woman began to leaf through lists of names. 'We have seen two English women. Here is one.' She held the list out, indicating an English name.

'Margaret Nichols,' Jake read. He shook his head. 'No. That's not her.'

He watched anxiously as the woman flicked through the papers again. 'No, sorry. The other one is called King.'

They thanked the woman and hurried outside again, into the early evening sunshine. 'What if Mum's not here, Jake?' Olly said, desperately.

'She will be.' Jake tried to sound reassuring, though he was just as frightened as Olly. He took Olly's hand and they darted through the crowd to the next building. Through the two large windows on either side of the door, Jake could see about fifteen people sitting at tables.

'It's just another café,' Olly said glumly. 'She won't be in here.'

Jake hesitated. Though there was a menu beside the door, nobody was eating or drinking. In fact, everyone seemed to be on the phone. 'I think it's an office,' he said.

The woman who sat nearest the door looked up and smiled at Jake and Olly. 'Let's go in,' Jake said. 'They might know where Mum is.'

They pushed the door open and went inside. The woman beckoned to them. They went across to her and waited, tensely, while she finished her phone conversation.

'Do you speak English?' Jake asked, when she finally replaced the receiver.

The woman called to the man at the next desk. He came over.

'Do you speak English?' Jake asked, again.

'Yes. What can I do for you?'

'We're trying to find our mother.'

'Is she here, in the evacuation centre?'

Jake shook his head. 'I don't know. She

was in the rain forest when the fire started.'
There was a map spread out on the table. He
bent over it and pointed out the area where
the protest camp was located. 'We were
camping around here.'

The man looked grave. 'That's close to
where the fire started.' He perched on the
corner of the desk. 'We're co-ordinating the
rescue of people trapped by the fire. We have
six search and rescue helicopters in the area,
flying along the river. There are also nine
boats. They're bringing people back all the
time. If your mother got to the river she'll
probably have been picked up.'

'Do the helicopters bring everybody
here?' Jake asked.

The man nodded. 'Unless they need to go
to hospital. Then they are taken straight to
Manaus.'

Olly slipped his hand into Jake's. Jake
glanced down at him. He was very pale and
his bottom lip was trembling.

'We've rigged up a Tannoy system here,'
the man said. 'Do you want me to put out a
call for your mother?'

'Yes, please,' Jake cried eagerly. 'Can you
say we'll meet her outside the medical
centre?'

'Of course. Give me your names and your mother's name.'

Sarah and her family were waiting by the medical centre when Jake and Olly arrived. There was nobody with them.

'Any luck?' Sarah asked.

Jake shook his head. 'But they're going to put out a call for her.' He looked round, trying to spot the loudspeakers. There was one mounted on the wall of the medical centre, just above the red cross, and another on a post near the jetty.

'Try not to worry,' Sarah's dad said. 'I'm sure your mum will turn up.'

'Your attention please.' The loudspeakers crackled into life. 'Would Gill Weston please go to the medical centre, where Jake and Oliver are waiting for her.'

'She'll come now,' Olly said. 'She has to.' He looked round, hopefully.

The message was repeated twice, then the loudspeakers fell silent again.

Jake sprang up on to the wall again so he could see over the heads of the crowd. Any moment now . . . he told himself. Any moment now, she'll come running along the road.

'Help me get up, Jake,' Olly said. 'I want to see Mum coming, too.'

Before Jake could move, Sarah's mother lifted him on to the wall. 'We'll wait with you until your mum comes,' she said.

Jake smiled. 'Thank you.'

Half an hour passed. People went in and out of the medical centre. The last two firefighters' helicopters took off. Boats came and went at the jetty, stopping just long enough to fill up with people before heading for Manaus. Jake paced up and down on the wall, too anxious to keep still.

'Where is she?' Olly wailed. 'Where is she?'

Jake slid an arm round his shoulders. 'I don't know.' Cold dread was stealing over him. She wasn't going to come. He was almost certain of that now. She wasn't going to come because she wasn't here. He shuddered. She might still be in the forest, desperately trying to escape from the fire. Or she could be in hospital. Or . . . An icy hand clutched his heart. She could be dead.

'Are you cold, Jake?' Sarah's mum asked. 'Perhaps we can find you a T-shirt from somewhere.'

He shook his head. 'I'm OK, thanks.' But he wasn't OK. He was very far from OK.

'What about your burns? Don't you think we ought to get you to the medical centre?'

'No. Honestly, I'm OK.' His burns were stinging like fury but he wasn't going to get them treated now, when his mum could turn up at any moment.

'Olly, show me where the office is,' Sarah's mum said. 'We'll ask them to put the Tannoy message out again.'

'Good idea,' her father said. 'Hannah and I will come with you.'

He lifted Olly down and they vanished into the crowd.

A helicopter appeared in the distance. Heart thumping, Jake watched it approach. It hovered above the field for a moment before descending. 'She might be in that helicopter,' he said to Sarah. He jumped down from the wall and ran towards it on trembling legs.

The helicopter touched down. The door opened. Jake edged forward, his heart thumping. A long-haired, dark-skinned man climbed out. He ducked low, to avoid the rotor blades, and ran across the grass. Jake looked past him, impatient to see who else was on board.

The man stopped, then came towards Jake. 'Jake? Jake Weston?'

Jake's stomach flipped over.

It was Paulo.

But his mum wasn't with him!

'Where's Mum?' He clenched his fists and pressed his lips tightly together, trying not to cry.

'She's in Manaus.'

'In hospital?' A cold shiver ran down Jake's spine.

Paulo nodded. 'But she's OK, Jake. She fell over as we were running from the fire and broke her wrist.'

Jake stared at him. 'She's not badly burnt?'

'No. She has burns too but she'll be overjoyed to know you're all right.' He frowned and looked around. 'Is Oliver with you?'

Jake nodded. He couldn't trust himself to speak. There was a massive lump in his throat and his eyes were wet with tears.

Sarah ran up to them and smiled warmly at Paulo.

Paulo patted Jake's shoulder. 'I'm glad you all made it.'

Jake smiled through his tears. 'So what happens now?' he asked.

'First we ring the hospital and get a message to Gill to say that you're both OK.

Then you and Oliver get on a boat to Manaus so you can see her. I'm going back into the rain forest with a team of firefighters to help put the fire out.'

'Will it take long?' asked Sarah.

Paulo shrugged. 'Sometimes a forest fire can burn for weeks. Sometimes, with enough help, and a bit of luck, it can be put out in days.' He looked up at the sky. 'Maybe it will rain tonight. Or tomorrow. This drought has to break soon.'

Jake thought of the forest creatures that must have died in the fire and of all the wildlife habitats that had been lost. 'It's such a waste,' he said. 'All those animals and plants wiped out.'

'The forest will grow back eventually,' Paulo said. 'It will take a long time before it's as good as it was but plants will come back. And the animals.' He smiled encouragingly. 'The fire isn't the end of everything, you know. And Maria and me and other protesters who care will be here to look after things.'

'Jake!'

Jake turned. Olly was stumbling towards him, his face alight with hope.

'Mum's OK, Olly,' Jake called. 'She's OK.'

★

The boat to Manaus was getting ready to leave. All the seats were taken and more people were sitting on suitcases or on the wooden deck. Two crew members were untying the ropes that fastened the boat to the jetty. Olly was squeezed into a seat near the stern. Jake stood by the rail.

'Write and let me know how your mum is, when you get back to England,' Sarah said. She was standing on the jetty.

'OK.' Jake nodded. 'What time do you think you'll get away?'

'Some time tomorrow evening by the look of this queue.' She laughed. 'Shame we couldn't all push in.'

Jake smiled. A place had been found for him and Olly on a boat so they could be reunited with their mother. He'd been allowed to jump the queue at the medical centre too, so that his burns could be treated before he left.

He smiled. 'It's funny to think that we came here to save the rain forest from loggers and that, in the end, it was a fire that destroyed everything.'

The boat's engine revved hard and the boat began to glide away from the jetty. The two crewmen leaped aboard.

'Stay in touch,' Sarah called, as she waved goodbye. 'And maybe, next holidays, we can get together again at a protest.' She laughed for the first time in two days.

Jake grinned. 'Only if it's in a cold, wet field somewhere in Britain.'

FIRE STORM

THE ESSENTIAL SURVIVAL GUIDE

Fire is unpredictable, destructive and completely natural.

Large-scale fires can have explosive effects on a massive scale. If you encounter one, you could expect:

●

Incredible heat that can reach temperatures of up to 1,655°C (3,011°F)

●

Suffocating clouds of poisonous smoke that blind and choke

●

Flames that behave unpredictably, consuming the air around you

●

Incredible damage – even concrete and metal will not be left untouched

●

Mass panic as the fire spreads at great speed

●

Terrifying noise that can disorientate and deafen

FIRE CONSUMES EVERYTHING

Warnings

There are no obvious warning signs that a fire is about to begin. Ideally, fires should be prevented. The safest way to do this is to make sure that flammable material does not come into contact with a heat source. But once a fire has started, your own eyes, ears and nose can usually detect the most obvious warning signs.

● **Sight** – Bright flames and smoke easily catch your eye, even at great distances.

● **Sound** – When a fire burns, it can create a great deal of noise: wood crackles, paint pops and flames roar.

● **Smell** – Within seconds, you will be aware of the pungent smoke produced by a fire, if it is close by.

● Smoke alarms can buy vital extra minutes for those at risk. The rapid high-pitched noise gives an early warning in thousands of homes and places of work around the world, making it possible to extinguinsh a fire before it takes hold and increasing the chances of escape.

Some fires involving natural gases like hydrogen burn without smoke. Without nature's usual warning signs, these fires are very difficult to spot.

Meltdown!

We live in a very flammable world and big fires can start almost anywhere. It's not always possible to avoid the danger, particularly if an escape route is not available.

If you are caught by a fire:

Get out of the way.
Inside buildings, quickly locate the nearest fire escape. If you are outside, forest fires can be fanned by the wind – so try to be aware of which direction it is coming from. Try to remain sensitive to the direction the fire is going. It may change. If you know where the fire has started, do your best to avoid it!

Raise the alarm.
At the first hint of a fire, raise the alarm. Contact the emergency services as soon as possible.

Where are you?
Think for a moment about where you are. Get your bearings, then act.

Take your time.
Move quickly, but do not rush. Try not to panic. If you do, you may behave rashly, increasing your risk of injury.

Protect yourself!
If possible, cover your face with a damp handkerchief

4

or cloth. It will offer some protection from fumes and searing heat.

Stay awake!
The fumes may start to make you feel drowsy. Try to stay alert. Splash cold water on your face, or pinch yourself.

Hot Tip
Don't be tempted to prop open fire doors. If you do, you will only encourage the fire to spread.

DO NOT try to fight the fire unless it is contained in a small area.

DO NOT open a door that feels hot in a building that is on fire. The fire is very likely to be behind it!

DO NOT stand upright when making your way through a smoky area. Smoke and heated gases rise. They are thinnest near floor level, so it will be easier to breathe if you crouch. Move quickly, but keep as low as you can.

DO NOT run if your clothes catch alight. Running will only fan the flames. Roll on the floor to try to smother the burning areas.

DO NOT return to a burning building.

DO NOT use lifts in a fire.

It is possible to extinguish a fire by removing one or more of the three essential ingredients:

With all three ingredients, fire burns

Suffocation: remove oxygen and fire dies

Starvation: remove fuel and fire dies

Cooling: if fire is cooled sufficiently, it dies

FIGHTING FIRES

Firefighters are usually the first to tackle large fires. They are experts and, in addition to extinguishers, they use other specialist equipment, which includes:

An air cylinder and face mask – vital in enclosed spaces and even outdoors where fumes from fires become thick or choking. Smoke sometimes contains carbon monoxide and other poisonous gases.

Fire-resistant suits – treated clothing designed to reflect heat. Firefighters use these for protection when tackling any large blaze.

A ceiling hook – a long pole with a hook and long blade used for turning off electrical equipment and pulling down smouldering debris from ceilings.

An axe – can be used for cutting a path into a burning building or to chop up debris to free a fire victim.

A sledgehammer – to punch holes in wood, plaster and plasterboard – either making a break for the fire or enabling the firefighter to reach someone.

A crowbar – for leverage to clear an obstruction.

A rope – used in the open to drag away partly burning objects or for pulling people clear of flames.

A power saw – a must out of doors, especially during forest emergencies. It is used to cut a path through to or away from runaway fires.

A pair of bolt cutters – snips wire, chains and other metal restraints to gain access to the fire.

A powerful fan – can be used to change the direction of a smaller fire.

7

A first-aid kit – containing plasters, bandages, disin-fectant creams or liquids, along with linament, pads, gauze and sprays to desensitize burns.

Water
(Red)

Extinguishers

There are four standard types of fire extinguisher: water, foam, liquid gas and dry powder. Three should be used only for specific types of fire. Be careful. Using the wrong extinguisher on the wrong type of fire can make things worse.

● Water – for burning solids, such as wood or cloth
● Foam – for liquid fires, such as petrol or paint, but not chip or fat pan fires
● Liquid Gas – for fires involving electrical equipment
● Dry Powder – for multipurpose use on all types of fires apart from chip or fat pan fires

If a person is on fire, the most effective way to put it out is to roll them in a fire blanket on the ground. The emergency services should be called immediately.

Burns

Heat and flames can quickly do terrible damage to the human body. There are three types of burn injury – from the first to the third degree.

Foam   Liquid Gas   Dry Powder   Fire Blanket
(Cream)   (Black)   (Blue)

First-degree burns

Also commonly known as 'scalds', these damage
the outer layer of skin, which goes red. Minor burns
can usually be treated by running the burned or
scalded area under cold water for about ten minutes until it has cooled.

Second-degree burns

These reach the second layer of skin and cause
blisters. Initially, they can be treated using a clean
towel or handkerchief soaked in cold water or holding the burn under a running cold tap, as described
above. Take off items like watches or jewellery
before the area begins to swell. Ideally, second-
degree burns should be treated by a doctor. If that
isn't possible and the blisters have burst, the injury
should be covered with a smooth sterile dressing.
You could use cling film or a clean plastic bag if
nothing else is available. Fluffy material would stick
to damaged skin, which is why the dressing must
be smooth.

Third-degree burns

These are the most serious. The fatty tissue and nerves below the skin are damaged. Anyone who has suffered third-degree burns must receive specialist medical attention as soon as possible. Treatment will almost certainly be in a hospital burns unit and include a course of fluid injections, skin grafts and even plastic surgery.

Fires - The Facts

What?

Fire is a chemical reaction involving oxygen and combustible substances.

Where?

Fires can start almost anywhere and can be man-made or natural.

Natural fires are most likely to occur in the drier grasslands and forested parts of the world, such as Australia, the tropical jungles of the Far East, the Amazon jungle, the coastal regions around the Mediterranean and the dry east and west coast areas of the USA.

Man-made fires most often happen as a result of an accident or human error, but many are caused deliberately by arsonists. They can occur almost anywhere, anytime.

When?

Natural fires occur most often during dry seasons

and the summer months: from June to August in the northern hemisphere and from December to February in the southern hemisphere. Natural bush fires in equatorial regions can occur at any time of the year.

How?
Fire needs three ingredients: oxygen, heat and fuel. A fire can be lit by a tiny spark, by lightning, by the concentration of the sun's rays, or by a large build-up of heat. All fires fuel themselves by vaporizing available solids or liquids until extinguished. Heat will radiate from the centre of the fire.

Effect?
Fire is often deadly and always extremely destructive, whether on a small or a large scale.

Many cities – from Ancient Tokyo to Dresden in war-torn Germany – have been virtually wiped out by fire. In the natural world, major fires can affect whole ecosystems, including even the atmosphere itself. However, as well as destruction, fires can also bring benefits. Natural fires can help in the regeneration of forests and pasture by stimulating new growth because ash is very good for the soil.

Man-made Fires

The British Safety Council and fire services recognize four main classes of fire in homes or places of work – Class A, B, C and D.

11

Class A – involving solid combustible materials such as cloth, paper, rubber and wood.
Class B – involving flammable liquids such as cooking fat, oil and petrol.
Class C – involving flammable gases.
Class D – involving flammable metals, such as magnesium.

Speed

A fire can take hold and spread incredibly quickly. It can take as little as four minutes for a fire to completely destroy a room. And something as small as a smouldering cigarette can start it.

Fireballs

During a fire in an enclosed space, such as a building, most material can become hot enough to catch light instantaneously. This phenomenon is known as flashover. In moments, the entire space can be consumed by flames. For flashover to occur, temperatures must reach at least 1,000°C (1,832°F). This 'fireball' can travel at up to 50 kph (31 mph) and firefighters call flashover 'The dance of the angels'.

Backdraught

In an enclosed or confined space, fire is kept alive by the air around it. If the air runs out and a fresh supply suddenly becomes available, for example by a window being opened, the fire explodes towards the fresh supply of air. This phenomenon is called backdraught.

How backdraught occurs

Fire burns in an unventilated room until the available oxygen is used up.

Fire, starved of oxygen dies down, leaving other combustible gasses still in the room ...

... then a door or a window is opened.

Oxygen rushes into the room, combining with unburnt gasses creating an explosive effect.

13

Forest Fires

Forest fires destroy huge swathes of dry and tropical woodland every year. They are sometimes started deliberately, but more frequently they occur naturally. These fires often begin on the forest floor and then rip upwards through the trees. In very dry woodland, fire can reach along the highest branches and spread across to other trees nearby.

Forest fires can spread in a variety of directions. They quickly get out of control unless checked.

● Many forests and woods have firebreaks – areas deliberately left bare and unplanted between the groups of trees. Firebreaks prevent the fire from 'jumping' a gap and spreading to adjoining areas.

● Most forests have lookout towers making it easier to see early signs of fire.

● Aircraft regularly patrol some areas in an attempt to spot small fires.

● Beaters, usually brushes made of twigs, will damp down small fires and stop them from spreading.

● Fire crews will create firebreaks, if none already exists when combating a large fire, by controlled burning of an area of woodland.

● Bulldozers are used to create large dampened-down breaks of soil or sand to prevent fire spread.

14

Firestarters!

Arson is one of the most deadly, dangerous and destructive crimes in the world. Never start a fire deliberately!

Fires - The Biggies

Place: London
Date: September 1666
London baker John Farynor was a careless man. On the night of the disaster, he went to bed in Pudding Lane, but forget to put out the fire in his ovens. Early the next morning, sparks set alight a pile of hay next door. What followed was London's biggest fire for the next three hundred years – until the Blitz of the Second World War. At first nothing was done – small fires were common at that time. But as it took hold and reached the warehouses along the River Thames, this fire became something bigger than anything Londoners had seen before. In all, 13,000 houses, fifty-seven churches and many businesses and shops were burned out. The old St Paul's Cathedral was left a ruin. The current building

wasn't re-built until 1710. Eventually, firebreaks were created by knocking down buildings and the fire was stopped.

Place: USS *Forrestal* aircraft carrier, off North Vietnam
Date: July 1967
Disaster struck the third largest ship in the US Navy when it was in hostile waters off the Vietnamese coast. Fourteen planes were about to take off (each with 5,000 lbs of explosives on board) when a fire was seen to one side of the planes. Fire and smoke covered the ship within minutes and the explosions were heard a quarter of a mile away. The disaster left 134 people dead and thirty-two injured. Sixty-three of the eighty-two planes aboard were destroyed or damaged, and the financial loss was estimated at $100 million. It took fourteen hours to put out all the fires aboard.

Place: São Paulo, Brazil
Date: February 1974
When a fire began on the eleventh floor of the Joelma office building, 220 people were killed. Within seconds, 650 people above the eleventh floor of the skyscraper were cut off. The fire then spread to the floors that they were on and those trapped went further and further up the building until they were out of reach of the fire service lad-

ders and faced certain death. Many decided to commit suicide by jumping. The rescue attempt was shown live on TV, while thousands ran into the streets to watch – more than 300,000 cars were abandoned, blocking all routes for the ambulances and firemen. Helicopters could not reach all those who were stranded because the flames and smoke were too strong.

Place: Australia
Date: February 1983
In temperatures reaching 43°F, bush fires began to sweep Australia on 16 February 1983. A strong wind fanned the flames into giant fireballs among the gumtrees near the city of Adelaide. More than 2,000 houses were eventually destroyed. The fire was so hot in one service station that a car became welded to machinery and the glass insulators on the telegraph poles melted into beads. Across the whole of Australia, 335,000 sheep and 18,000 cattle were destroyed. The fire caused a cloud of dust which was so thick that it turned a bright day into night in the state of Victoria. Eventually the fire was put out by rain.

Ten of the worst peacetime fires

(Ranked in order of death toll)

1670 dead   **May 1845**
Canton theatre, China

1182 dead   **October 1871**
Peshtigo forest, Wisconsin, USA

850 dead   **December 1881**
Ring theatre, Vienna, Austria

602 dead   **December 1903**
Iroquois theatre, Chicago

500+ dead   **December 1995**
Mandi Dabwali school, India

491 dead   **November 1942**
Cocoanut Grove nightclub,
Boston, USA

480 dead   **September 1894**
Forest fire, Minnesota, USA

439 dead   **October 1913**
Mid-Glamorgan colliery, Wales

425+ dead   **August 1978**
Abadan cinema, Iran

323 dead   **December 1961**
Niteroi circus, Brazil

Against the Odds

Survivors of fires often owe their lives to quick-thinking, sheer endurance or plain good luck – sometimes all three!

During the Triangle company fire in New York on 25 March 1911, a young man saved three girls by holding them out into the air from the ninth floor of the burning building. He then let them fall to be caught by the firemen below.

In the great Australian Bush fire of 1983, the Johns family had left behind their pet rabbit when evacuating to safety. While their house was burned to the ground, the rabbit was found the next morning on the back lawn eating a carrot!

During a fire in 1983 at Macedon, Australia, a mother and her two children took shelter in a duck pond. As the fire burned down their home, they sang 'Twinkle, Twinkle, Little Star'. They survived and were later rescued by a neighbour.

19

A few survived the fire at the Cocoanut Grove night-club in Boston, America, by locking themselves in the refrigeration room. After their rescue, two of the survivors who became hysterical were knocked out by a nurse who knew ju-jitsu!

George Sellar was one of sixteen people trapped by flames in the bushfire at Matlock, Australia in 1939. He soaked a blanket in water, wrapped himself in it and sucked air through it. He was the only one of the sixteen to survive.